Saving Eden

By K. R. S. McEntire

Created with Vellum

Chapter One

The midnight air made goose bumps rise on Angela's arm as she climbed out the cabin window onto the branches of the nearby tree. Careful not to make a sound, she made her way down its trunk until her bare feet sank into the cool, damp ground.

Angela wasn't allowed outside at night. She welcomed the adrenaline that surged through her, unable to remember the last time she had done anything deliberately disobedient. She took a deep breath, but did not stand idle. If there were any hope of completing her mission, she would have to move quickly.

Daring herself to breach the fence that marked her boundary line, the moon was her only source of light as she struggled to make her way through the massive garden that had been reduced to shadows.

Angela crept through the dark until something hard hit her shin. She yelped and stumbled towards the ground, her hands and face crashing on the cold, wet dirt. She swiped at the mud that stained her clothes and glanced back at the cabin, cursing herself for being so loud.

Angela scowled at the backpack that caused her fall. She dragged it over, reaching inside. She could tell what was in the pack by shape and texture alone: smooth apples, rough potatoes, and berries crushed by the weight of the larger fruits and vegetables.

She wondered why her father would put food in a pack, then realized that the backpack's shape and color were unfamiliar. Her heart began to race — she *knew* the sounds that she had been hearing at night could not have come from a woodland animal. Angela had long been doubtful that she and her father were truly the last two people alive on earth. There was someone out here, sneaking about at night and stealing their food. With this new discovery alone, Angela felt her investigation was fruitful.

Angela scanned the garden with her eyes. If this pack was still here, she thought, it was likely her visitor was nearby as well. She saw a swift movement in the distance and squinted, struggling to see by the light of the crescent moon. A tall shadowy figure raced through the garden and disappeared into the night. The dark silhouette stood on two legs and looked human. The bag fell from Angela's hand as she shrieked in shock.

She wondered if it was one of the monstrous mutants her father had warned her about — once-human creatures born of the earth's decay. From the corner of her eye, she noticed the glow of candle-light shining through the upstairs cabin window where her father, Nathan, slept. Before Angela had time to collect her thoughts and worry about his punishment for catching her outside at night, he had rushed downstairs and grabbed her shoulders from behind.

"Angela," he whispered, "are you okay? What are you doing out here?"

Angela spun around to face her father. When she saw concern in his eyes rather than anger, she felt guilty for sneaking out. She buried her head into his shirt and waited for her heart rate to return to normal.

"It's okay," he soothed, wrapping his arms around her like vines. Stroking her hair, he said. "Let's go back inside."

She allowed him to guide her back into their home, her prison. Placing a candle on the kitchen table, he took a good look at Angela—her curly black hair wild and her lean legs bruised from the fall.

"Why were you outside? What did you see?" he asked.

Angela was unable to look him in the eye. She knew the figure in the garden could mean danger, but all of her life was out in the open. The secret that there was something out there, some unknown creature that could be human, was the only knowledge she had to herself.

"I heard something. It must have been an animal. So I went outside to investigate," Angela said vaguely, knowing how rare finding any live animal, except for the occasional bird or squirrel, would be. Still, it was not nearly as uncommon as a six-foot-tall figure that could pass as human.

"I taught you better than to go wandering off at night, Angela. You worry me sometimes." His sincere tone deepened Angela's guilt.

"I was just curious. Anyway, I'm safe now, but I'm really tired. Can I go back to bed?" Angela asked.

Nathan nodded. Angela averted her eyes before walking back upstairs to her room. When her head hit her pillow, she found she could not drift off; her mind insisted on replaying the events that lead to her discovery.

Earlier that day, before Angela had dared to climb from her window into the night, her father had penalized her for looking at a picture she found in his room. The picture showed a woman with warm brown skin and dark, curly hair sitting on golden sand. Behind the woman, Angela saw gentle waves reaching towards the shore. The water held reflections of the sky above, brilliant and bright. It mirrored the sky's endless blue eternity. She figured this must be the ocean, though she only knew of the ocean from stories her father told about the world beyond the garden.

Angela was hit with the sudden realization of how beautiful the world must have been before biological warfare killed everyone off. It distressed her to know that she would never get the chance to dip her toes in the ocean or to speak with any other humans.

That was when Nathan barged into the room. Confusion filled his face at the sight of Angela rummaging through his things. His eyes flashed with anger as he realized what exactly she was looking at, but the anger was mixed with some other emotion that Angela could not identify.

"Angela!" he boomed. Hearing her father raise his

voice was unsettling. His demeanor was typically serene.

"Is this woman my mother?" Angela asked. She had never been shown a picture of her mother before, but the slim build, wild hair, and brown skin of the woman in the photograph matched her own reflection. She didn't inherit many of her father's features, save for his hazel eyes and stubborn nature.

Nathan didn't answer her question. Instead, he scolded her for going through his things. Defeated, Angela marched upstairs to her room. She slammed her door for dramatic effect and stayed put as the remainder of the day slipped into night.

She'd almost fallen asleep when she had heard it, for the third night in a row: a rustling in the bushes outside and a whistling that mirrored the notes of her favorite song.

There was someone in the garden.

Angela felt like a bird trapped in a cage, but she knew nighttime was the only time she could escape from her father's watchful gaze. That's why, under the cover of darkness, she'd decided to sneak out and discover the source of the sound. Now that she was back in the safety of her bed, she mentally scolded herself for screaming like a child at the sight of the stranger. Her father would have an increasingly watchful eye now that he knew she had snuck out once. She tried to envision new methods of investigation as she drifted off to sleep.

THE NEXT MORNING, ANGELA SOUGHT HER favorite form of therapy: music. She made her way outside to the grand piano that sat in the center of the vast garden surrounding their home.

She gently pressed a pencil that was half the size of her index finger onto a yellow-paged notebook to record a few notes. Angela knew that after things were gone, they could never be replaced. No matter how light her inscriptions were, the pencil would not last forever. Where would she store her compositions after her only way of recording it was gone?

Angela sighed as she looked toward the hand-built, two-story cabin. Every inch of their home had been carefully constructed, revealing how clever and capable her father was. His potential caused her to question why they lived the way they did, using only leftovers from long ago instead of venturing out and restocking their repository. Their way of existence didn't add up in Angela's mind.

She scanned their home with her eyes. Four fingers gripping the blue curtain of a downstairs window caught her attention. She saw one of

Nathan's eyes peek into the crack he had created to spy on her.

Angela quickly removed her gaze from the window to look at the bright sky. When she was sure he hadn't seen her watching him, she spun around on the wooden bench back towards the piano. She grinned as her fingers danced over the keys, the wind carrying the sound of her favorite song; the same tune she had been hearing the voice whistle at night.

She watched the curtain fall back into place, but kept the corner of her eye on the cabin door. It creaked open as Nathan's tall, round frame filled the doorway. His lips formed an awkward grin while he held in one hand what appeared to be a balled-up newspaper. Angela let him walk halfway to where she was seated before she looked up and acknowledged him.

"What is it?" Angela asked, playing the last notes of her song as he approached the piano.

She shook her head at the sight of Nathan's usual clothing: a pair of faded jeans with a once-white t-shirt that was now tinted brown from grime and use. It was full of holes that he hadn't bothered to mend. She couldn't comprehend how he could believe they were the last people on the planet and yet never consider leaving their home base to look for clothes and supplies.

"It's nothing. Just...you've gotten so big," he said.

"Didn't happen overnight," Angela replied dryly, a smirk forming on her lips.

"I have something for you," he said, holding out what looked like a round bundle of newspapers, held together with tape.

Angela took it, unwrapping and storing the paper in her dress pocket. Her father was oblivious to the fact that her favorite part of his makeshift birthday gifts was the old newspaper pages he used as wrapping paper. She could not read them, but she enjoyed looking at pictures of people and places and imagining the former world.

Inside the paper was a golden watch, its three hands unmoving against the shining face.

"It was your mother's," Nathan explained. "It's broken and a little big for your wrist, but maybe you'll grow into it...happy sixteenth birthday, Angela."

Her father slipped the watch on her wrist and tightened it. Angela glanced at the similar contraption on his wrist. The hands on his watch were still slowly ticking, but Angela couldn't help but think her father's watch was just as useless. She glanced at both contraptions and frowned. When would they ever need to use one of these in a barren, dead world where they were the last people on earth?

"A watch, like yours," Angela said while touching

the object on her father's wrist, her index finger following the movement of its second hand. "But you've never taught me how to use one. They tell the time, right?"

"Yes, but the time doesn't matter, Angela," he pointed out. "It's the symbolism that matters. I'm sorry about how I acted last night. You have a right to look at a picture of your mother. I wanted you to have something that belonged to her."

He narrowed his gaze as she retrieved the newspaper from her pocket.

"Why won't you tell me what these symbols mean?" Angela said, trying to keep her tone light. She wished he would teach her how to read and write more than music notes. She wanted to tell time and read books, maybe even write them. She was too old to rely on begging him to read to her from the books inside the tattered cardboard boxes in his room. She knew he wasn't educating her on purpose, but the reason behind his secrecy was a mystery.

The wrinkles that appeared on his forehead let Angela know that her casual tone didn't fool him. He wasn't going to give in to her innocent interrogation.

"I have told you. They are stories," he answered, taking a seat beside her on the bench.

"A fairy tale?" asked Angela. She knew the plot to every fantastic tale her father shared with her before bedtime when she was younger. She adored stories about knights, princes, dragons, and good defeating evil. She longed to be transported to a world like that, to rescue someone in need or find her one true love. But the world beyond the garden gates was dead, and she knew her father's stories were not true.

Her father preferred reading her fiction books and fairy tales to sharing stories about the real world, but she had picked up bits and pieces of information about the world over time. She knew that there had been a series of wars. In addition to using bombs and bullets, armies had unleashed disease in the air, food, and water to kill their enemies. After the wars ended, food became scarce and what little there was to be found was often contaminated. Without food, people died off. Angela wasn't sure how her father had discovered the garden that they lived in, but here, nourishment was plentiful. He told her that having been in one place for so many years with no visitors or signs of life beyond the critters that took refuge in their garden meant there was a high possibility that no other humans were left. He wasn't willing to leave and risk death, just to confirm his theory.

Angela thought his perspective to be selfish. She didn't understand why, if he knew a safe place like this garden existed, he didn't bring others along. It felt as if her father had abandoned humanity for his own private paradise.

Despite the stillness of the woods that surrounded their home, Angela was not convinced they were the last people alive. She could tell by the lighthearted way he spoke the words, "there's no one else," that her father did not truly believe it either. Angela had always believed that there were people out there somewhere. The figure she saw last night had two legs and two arms; it sure *looked* human.

"It's just a newspaper," he frowned at her. "It's outdated, from thirteen years ago. Judging by how things were going then, I wouldn't want to see one from today. Of course, there are no people to make them anymore. It's a moot point."

Angela looked down at the ground, lost in her own mind. She wanted to understand what the letters on the paper said. It was hard to keep the things she felt from slipping out of her mouth and offending her father. She broke out of her daze-like state at the feel of his hand on her shoulder.

"With the way things were...I don't know if there's anything left to look forward to." He placed a hand under her chin, lifting her face so he could gaze into her eyes. "This place is probably the closest thing to a fairy tale that the world has left. This is our happy ending."

Angela averted her gaze.

"Thank you," she whispered politely.

He nodded before taking his leave. Angela watched as he made his way back inside the cabin and closed the door behind him. She took one last look at the undecipherable inscriptions on the newspaper before shoving it inside the pocket on her dress.

Angela had always hoped that one day she would wholeheartedly accept her father's limitations, but now that she knew for certain that there was something other than mutated birds and bugs out in the forest, she needed to find out what it could be. She desperately wanted whatever she had seen to come back. Angela continued to play her music, finding the tune was the only thing that could relax her. She would never be able to erase the figure she had seen in the garden from her memory.

DAYS WENT BY AND ANGELA SPENT HER NIGHTS watching the garden from her bedroom window until her eyes betrayed her and she fell asleep, but the shadowy figure did not return. Angela had plenty of time to fantasize about what or who it could have been. Her most whimsical guess was that it was her mother, miraculously alive and seeking to reunite with her long lost family.

A less optimistic part of her was starting to wonder if she had imagined the whole occurrence. It had been dark. The figure could have been one of the monsters her father had warned her about or some strange type of animal. The backpack, which she kept hidden under her bed, was her only reminder that the visitor was real.

Angela forced herself to forget about the visitor and her life fell back into its previous routine. Each day, Angela rose with the sun, ate a quick breakfast, and helped her father work in the garden.

In all honesty, garden was too modest a word for the thirty acres of growth and life they called home. From Angela's piano bench, she could enjoy the fluttering shade of a large apple tree's leaves and breathe in the sweet scent of flowers. She could watch bees float around the nearby assortment of fruits, vegetables, and herbs, and listen to the sound of water flowing steadily from the creek that provided them with an untainted supply of water. Nathan sometimes joked about having his own personal Garden of Eden, and Angela was left to wonder what he meant by that, seeing as she had been left in the dark about that particular story.

The cabin that her father had built for the two of

them was in the center of it all. Sitting about ten feet in front of the cabin was Angela's piano. He said that he found the piano abandoned in the forest and claimed it was the piano, not the garden, that inspired him to build the cabin and call this little slice of the world, "home." He played the piano as a child and felt it would be nice to teach Angela when she became old enough to learn.

Surrounding their home was a wooden fence, but a mass of tangled tree limbs blocked Angela's view of whatever lay beyond. She tried to imagine what wonders could be found inside a fenceless world that never stopped, but all she could see in the distance was vast emptiness, hills with brown grass and rotting trees.

After all their work was done, she spent her days crafting beautiful music. One night she stayed out later than usual. After playing her piano she decided that, rather than going inside for supper right away, she would stay out and watch the sun set. She was lying in the grass beside the piano with her eyes locked on the sky, when an eerie feeling crept upon her. She couldn't shake the sensation that she was not alone. She looked around and discovered a pair of unfamiliar eyes peering at her from behind a distant bush that failed to hide his form.

These light brown, astonished eyes belonged to a

boy, almost a man, in blue jeans and a black t-shirt. Though he was dirty and skinny, seeing this face was like seeing hope in human form. In his hands was a bundle of berries from her garden, the same kind that she had found smushed in the backpack that was currently hidden under her bed.

A mix of shock and excitement coursed through Angela's veins; her visitor was back. Now that she could see him clearly in the daylight, there was no mistaking that he was a human.

He looked weak, as if he had not eaten for many days. Had he been afraid to come back for food out of fear of seeing her again?

Angela smiled at him, hoping to learn more about her uninvited guest. Her smile seemed to break him out of his trance and he took off running back the way he came.

"Wait!" she called after him, but he didn't stop. His thin legs raced through her garden at an incredible pace for someone who appeared so fatigued.

Angela didn't know much about the outside world, but she couldn't let this opportunity pass. Her father was wrong. There *were* other people out there. She chased after him, racing through her garden as fast as she could force her legs to go. When he leaped over their wooden fence, she only hesitated a second before doing the same. Angela had so many questions, and this was the perfect time to get them answered.

It took Angela longer to propel her body over the gate. She was clearly not as practiced as her visitor. He was a good distance ahead of her now, and Angela worried he would disappear into the woods. Despite his agility, his foot hit an exposed root from a tree. She watched as he tripped and fell, hitting his head on a large rock. Angela froze in her tracks before cautiously walking over to where he lay.

"Are you okay?" Angela said when she finally caught up.

Having never met anyone besides her father, she hesitated about touching him. Cautiously, she placed her hand on his dirty cotton t-shirt. She could feel his chest rising and falling beneath her hand. There was a small amount of blood on his head. She gently shook him.

"Wake up," Angela whispered. She listened to the slow breaths struggling to escape his motionless body. She deliberated going home and asking her father for help but wasn't sure how he would respond to another human being here. Her father was likely to send him away. The idea of leaving this boy's side, even for a brief moment, was unbearable. So many questions danced inside of her head about the world beyond the garden. The only thing she knew for certain was that this magnificent stranger could finally give her the answers she craved.

"Please keep breathing. You can't die on me now." Angela's heart pounded hard against her chest as she hoped for a miracle.

Chapter Two

Angela stopped poking and shaking him after she realized that trying to wake him was doing absolutely nothing. Instead she sat with him, full of apprehension, and held his hand.

Being outside the garden put Angela on edge. Even though she was only a short walk away from her home, she felt as if she had entered a forbidden and dangerous world. Rather than the luscious plants and flowers that grew within their garden, the soil under her bare feet was hard and the brown grass struggled to rise from it. The branches on the trees bore no leaves, and the lack of shade caused the sun to sting her skin.

Angela inspected the boy. Blood and grime covered both his golden skin and the dark hair that fell halfway down his face. Despite his current state,

Angela found the smooth features of his face to be handsome.

Happiness bubbled up inside Angela when, after what felt like forever, she saw his eyes open weakly and heard him murmur something inaudible. She brimmed with energy, equal parts anticipation and fear.

"Hey!" she exclaimed. "How are you feeling?"

His body was still, but his eyes shifted to meet hers. The expression on his face was incredibly calm for someone who had blacked out for so long. Though the mass of tree limbs above him partially eclipsed his view of the setting sun, the exposed light that slithered through the branches caused him to squint. He could not see the worry etched on Angela's face.

"Music girl," he murmured, starting to close his eyes again.

"Please stay awake," Angela pleaded as she reached for him and touched his cheek, wiping grime away from his wounds. His eyes blinked open and he looked at Angela expectantly.

Angela suddenly felt shy. She had never spoken to anyone but her father before. She plucked at a loose string on the bottom of her dress and looked away as she spoke. "My dad says sleeping after you hit your head is a bad idea."

The boy sat up straighter now, placing his hand on his wounded head to survey the damage. He inspected his hand and wiped the blood on his jeans. He looked over at Angela.

"How did you find that place?" he asked with bewilderment in his voice. His voice, smooth and deep, sounded as good as music to Angela.

"I'm not really sure myself," Angela admitted. "I grew up here."

The boy looked over her homemade dress and her bare feet. He studied her facial expression for answers that he couldn't find, but his body relaxed as he realized that Angela wasn't going to hurt him.

"Beautiful," he finally said.

Angela's face grew warm. "Excuse me?"

"Your garden. It's beautiful, it looks completely unaffected," he finally said. "The soil is soft, the fruit tastes good. So much food."

"I'm not sure why this land is healthy," she admitted. "Not that I'm complaining."

"When I came out into the wilds, I didn't know what to expect. But definitely not this," he said. "I feel like I stepped into a time machine and entered the world our great-grandparents lived in."

Angela tilted her head to the side. Her father had a book about a time machine in his room. She assumed it was fiction, but now she was unsure. "You have a real time machine?"

Rather than answering Angela's question, the boy let out a burst of deep, hearty laughter. Angela wondered if he was delusional.

"If I did, I wouldn't be here," he said. "And how the hell did you get a piano out here?"

This caused Angela to giggle. She found it amusing that out of all things, he was curious about her piano. She did not know why her garden was healthy despite the barren land, and even if she did know, she wouldn't share that information with a stranger.

"You ask a lot of questions," Angela dodged. "But you still haven't shared what *you* are doing out here?"

"That's fair," he said. "My name's Jesse, and I'm out here because, despite their official job descriptions, the Wardens of the Watch seem more interested in keeping the community in the settlements than in hunting down people who get out. I ran away because it was safer for me to be out here."

While the majority of what he had said confused Angela, she understood that he had run away from a community of other people. It was hard to contain her excitement at the prospect of other survivors.

"Who are the Watch?" Angela looked around the forest to see if there were any other strangers around.

Jesse watched her face intently, trying to see if she was joking.

"Have you been living under a rock?" he finally asked.

Angela eyes grew wide with amazement, "Do people live under rocks where you are from?"

Jesse paused for a second, trying to pick up hints of sarcasm in Angela's voice.

"It's a figure of speech," Jesse took in Angela's blank expression. "Have you lived here forever?"

Angela shrugged, then folded her arms over her chest. "Pretty close, I guess."

He chuckled, "Well, it looks like you found yourself a pretty nice rock to live under. I don't understand how it hasn't been affected. I would apologize for stealing food . . . except if I didn't, I would not be alive to apologize so, sorry, not sorry. Survival of the fittest, you know?"

Angela giggled again. He seemed to speak in riddles. She had never heard the phrase, 'survival of the fittest,' but could guess at his meaning. He stole the food to stay alive.

"What's your name, and why do you live out here?" Jesse asked, breaking the silence.

"My name is Angela, and I live here because my father lives here," Angela said. "I didn't have much choice in the matter because I was three years old when we first came here. I don't remember anyplace else."

Angela didn't know what was going on with the outside world, but she had realized long ago that her father was afraid to leave their home. Maybe her father didn't know about the community that Jesse was from.

"Where are you planning to go?" Angela asked.

Jesse shrugged. "No destination, just hiding out and hoping for a miracle," he said, sitting up and resting his back against a nearby tree trunk. "Had a Warden look up my CitCard credentials, which were fake, so I had to leave the city for a bit. I didn't really have a destination until I heard music in the distance. I followed the sound, then I stumbled upon your garden. I've never seen anything like it."

Angela's eyes widened, "A real city? Like, with thousands of people all living together?"

He chuckled. "Not thousands, but there are about five hundred survivors in my city. I guess I should actually call it a settlement. The population is growing, now that more women are having children again. It may reach city status again."

Angela wanted to ask more questions about the settlement but decided her curiosity would have to wait. She knew her father's eyes would peek out of the curtains soon and he would not find her inside their gates. She didn't want him to notice her absence or to see the boy just yet. Now that Jesse was fully conscious, she had to leave him.

"I have to go check on my father. Will you wait for me here?" Angela asked.

"If you promise to bring me more food from the garden, I could be persuaded," Jesse replied.

Angela chuckled. "Deal. I'll be back as soon as possible."

Angela swore to bring him a plate after dinner.

ANGELA REMAINED RESTLESS ONCE SHE MADE IT back home. She knew so little about the events that lead to the world's demise. She wanted her questions answered, so she decided to do whatever she had to do to discover the truth.

"Daddy, I have a question," Angela walked up to her father that evening after dinner. He was sitting in his room, reading a tattered novel about a bandit in the Wild West that he had read ten times before.

His room consisted of a window, a small desk, two chairs and a bed, all made of wood and, though ancient, had been cared for over the years. Boxes of his belongings lined the walls. Angela felt most of his things were unimportant here, just leftovers from a former world. Mementos. She had rummaged through most of his items years ago, tried on a pair of sunglasses, opened a birdcage, pressed the buttons of a calculator. To Angela, they were artifacts from an old, forgotten tomb.

"What is it?" he asked without looking up.

Angela walked over to where he was seated and quietly pulled up a chair, hoping he would realize that they were about to have a serious conversation.

"Why did you leave your home, wherever we lived before, and come here?" Angela asked. She waited for answers or anger.

He put the book on his desk. "And what inspired your sudden burst of curiosity?"

Angela wondered how much she should reveal about her guest. Maybe if her father knew that there were other people out there, he would want to venture beyond the garden with her. At the same time, she didn't want to alarm her father or get Jesse into trouble.

"That night, when I heard a noise and went outside, I found a backpack in the garden with our food in it. It wasn't one of our backpacks." Angela took a moment to gauge her father's reaction. His rosy face turned a ghostly white.

"That is concerning. Why didn't you tell me this until now?" he asked.

"I didn't want to bring up sneaking out again," Angela said. "But I want to be informed on what could be out there, for safety. I was wondering who, or what, brought us here?"

"It was because that is what's best for you and your future," he said. "You can see that everything else is dead. Everything I have done has been for you."

"What future?" Angela asked with more passion in her voice than she meant to let out. "If there are other people out there—"

"Our life is perfect. You could not have had it better living anywhere else," he said, "We have food, shelter, peace—"

"But what if they don't?" Angela asked. "What if there are others out there, whoever had the backpack, and what if the others need our help?"

Nathan's lips formed a tight line, "I have read you too many fairy tales, and now you dream of being a hero and saving this world. But the real world has teeth, and its sickness reaches far beyond the aftermath of war. If there are other survivors, I know nothing about them. I have been here with you, trying to give you a better life."

"I think you are right about one thing," Angela said. "You have read me too many fairy tales. So maybe it's time you tell me a true story."

Angela knew her next question was likely to trigger the anger she was preparing herself for. "I want to know more about what happened to my mom."

Angela saw her father's lips press together again. The tone of his voice darkened, "Your mother was a great woman, Angela. Kind hearted, free spirited, and trusting, but everybody was getting sick and your mother wasn't immune. The doctor said she had three months to live. Two days later, we found out she was pregnant with you."

"But . . . how—" Angela was confused. Angela had inquired about the process of bringing new life into the world years ago, and she knew it took more than three months to carry a child.

Nathan cupped his hands together and looked at Angela intently. He seemed to be choosing his words carefully.

"The biological warfare was making people sick, and every self-appointed scientist or sage had a miracle cure-all for desperate people to try. And we were desperate people. She tried so many experimental drugs while she was pregnant with you . . . stuff said to heal the body and mind. Most of those "cures" only caused addictions or sped up the process of death. Some causes genetic mutations, or made the user to go mad. But for your mother, it seemed to be working. For a while, at least. She started to gain her strength back and carried you to term. I allowed myself to gain hope that we could be a family. But a week after you were born, she died."

Angela didn't know what to say, so she looked down at her feet and waited for him to continue.

"Angela, the way the world was at that time, everyone was getting sick in many ways. I'm not just talking about the physical illnesses. I think people's souls were sick as well. People became violent, especially towards those with mutations. All of the happy endings have been played up. They only exist in books, that is why I teach you better stories."

"I think sometimes you have to create a happy ending yourself," Angela stated.

Nathan exhaled noisily as a hopeless expression filled his face, "Angela, don't you understand? I loved your mother and I could not keep her safe, I will not make the same mistake with you. We are healthy, and food is growing here. This place is our happy ending, Angela. We are free from all of that now."

"Maybe this place is your ending, but it's not mine," Angela said. "If you knew someone else was alive, wouldn't you want to help them?"

"No," Nathan said. "If there is one thing I have learned over the years, it's that people can't be trusted." His eyes did not look up from the closed book on his desk. His body was tense, his voice agitated.

"Angela, go outside and play your music. Doesn't that make you happy?" He spoke quickly, "You should be thankful for all that you have here."

"Okay." Angela realized this was as far as this conversation was going to go. He did not want to help Jesse. She had her answer. "And I am thankful, really. I just wanted to know if there were people who need our help. I just want to do what is best for the world."

Her father reached out and put his hand on her shoulder. "The world is dead. What's best for you is that you stay here. Trust me."

Angela was too fatigued to argue. She felt as if she had been lied to her entire life, now that she had proof the world was alive. She could not stay here forever, but she knew Nathan would never leave or let her go—not unless she could prove to him that there was someplace worth going. She knew what she had to do next.

Chapter Three

Late that night, after Nathan fell asleep, Angela crept down to the kitchen and poured leftover soup from dinner into a bowl. Then, to avoid opening the front door, she went back upstairs and escaped through her window as swiftly as the breeze blew in. Soup splashed onto her arm as she climbed down the tree, and she felt guilty for not bringing him food while it was still hot. She crept through the garden and ventured into the forest.

"Hey!" Angela called while trampling through the woodlands. "You can stop hiding now."

Her garden was always full of the sounds of birds chirping, squirrels climbing and water flowing, but the forest was eerily quiet; she didn't hear a single bird, bee, or cricket. The moon cast shadows between the bare, willowy trees.

In the darkness, the forest looked unfamiliar. She had been so excited when she met Jesse that she had forgotten to make note of any landmarks. Not that there was much to use as a landmark. All of the trees, rocks, and roots around her were indistinguishable. She froze in her tracks and looked around. Had she wandered too far? Her stomach twisted with dread.

"Hey!" she called out. "I have soup!"

As she stumbled through the forest into unknown territory she wondered if Jesse had gone back to his home. Her heart sank at the thought of it.

While she pondered the possibility of Jesse having run off, she heard a twig snap from behind her, the tiny sound might as well have been a loud boom in the quiet woods. Heart pounding, she spun around to face the sound, but no one was there.

"Jesse?" she called, looking over her shoulder to make sure whatever had made that noise wasn't coming towards her from behind. While her father never mentioned the possibility of people living beyond their garden, he had warned her about the mutants. The biological warfare had caused some humans and animals to evolve in frightening new ways. Her father had a pistol with a single bullet in case one of the monsters decided to invade their home.

The bushes around her started to rattle, but she couldn't make out which direction the sound was coming from. She stood, her heart racing, holding Jesse's soup as she waited for whatever was coming to find her.

A moment later, Jesse stumbled out of the wilderness. Angela heaved a sigh of relief.

"Soup?" he asked, his eyes locked on the food in her hands.

Angela laughed as she handed over the bowl. As he ate hungrily, she sat next to him, looking him over. The blood was gone, but a nasty-looking scab was forming on his temple. Angela noticed that he was never completely relaxed; he was always looking over his shoulder to make sure no one was there. Every once in awhile he would glance over at her with curiosity in his eyes.

"I noticed you never wear shoes," he said when his soup was halfway finished.

"I was three when I came here. I outgrew them," Angela said, brushing off his question. "Besides, the soil in our garden is much softer than anything out here. I want to know more about you. You mentioned a city. What's it called?"

The questions caused Jesse to tense up a bit.

"Chicago," he said. Angela didn't know where or what Chicago was, but she nodded anyway.

"So how do you get there...to Chicago?" Angela asked.

"You want to go to Chicago?" he asked skeptically, chuckling.

"I think I do, if there are other people like you there," she said thoughtfully. "My father and I have more food than we could ever eat. Do the people in Chicago have food?"

Jesse leaned back against a tree trunk. "We do, but not nearly enough for all of the people within the settlement limits. There are a few independent farmers in our community, but for the most part, the Watch controls the food supply."

Angela frowned. There was that word again—Watch. He clearly wasn't talking about the object on her wrist. But who were they watching?

"Tell me about the Watch," Angela said.

"Public enemy number one," Jesse replied. "President Kane's lackeys."

"President." Angela was happy to have heard a familiar word. Her father told her about presidents. As a country's leader, they reminded her of the rulers in her favorite fairy tales.

"Like a king," Angela said.

This caused Jesse to laugh out loud. "Kane's no king. He's not even really the president. We don't have a true government anymore and we don't have elections. His family was the richest family to survive the Bio Wars. They own land outside of the states. Uncontaminated land. When you have resources in a world without any you can call yourself anything you want. Kane's a man who gave himself a title and he had enough money that no one questions it. He controls the shipments of food and supplies that go to each settlement's community. He also issued the CitCards that hold our money."

"How do you get to the settlement?" asked Angela.

"Well Chicago, or what's left of it, is a little over two weeks' walk away. But you can't just go frolicking in," he said.

Two weeks' walk? Angela thought. All this time, she was only *two weeks* away from where hundreds of other people lived? Angela was surprised other humans had been so close, yet had never found her garden until now.

"Why can't I walk in?" she asked.

"That's much too dangerous. If you want to get in, you need one of these." He pulled a small, plastic object out of his pocket and held it out in front of her. It had a picture of Jesse's face on it, minus the mud and scabs, and words that Angela could not read.

"I'm sorry, I don't understand what it is," she admitted.

"It's a citizenship card, or CitCard for short," he said. "At least it looks enough like one for me to get by."

Angela nodded, figuring she could quiz him about the tiny object later. She had more pressing questions to ask. "Why did you run away? Is there something . . . dangerous . . . in the settlement?"

A smile tugged on the corners of Jesse's lips. "Of course the settlement is dangerous, but that's not why I ran away. I did something that tore me up inside, and I came out here to redeem myself. Sometimes, it's hard to find peace without a little chaos."

Angela knew this was all too true. The reason she had never questioned Nathan before was to keep the peace.

"Elaborate," Angela pressed.

"It's a long story," Jesse continued. "There were some Wardens on my tail, and I had to lay low for a bit. But, I think my journey is coming to an end soon. I have been gone for a whole month. They will probably assume I am dead. When you found me, I was trying to stock up on food for the journey home. I was wondering if you could help me with that? Could you get some food from your garden for me? I plan on leaving tomorrow, in the night."

Angela's eyes grew wide.

"Tomorrow!" she exclaimed. "But . . . you just got here."

"Technically, I've been here for a while. You just didn't notice me," he said. "I'm feeling a lot better now, and I really should get back."

Leaving tomorrow, Angela thought, realizing it was now or never. She forced herself to ask a question that terrified her, "Can you take me with you when you go back?"

There was silence. Jesse looked skeptical. Finally, he asked, "Why would you want me to do that? You live here with your father and I'm not a kidnapper."

"I'm not a kid," Angela responded.

Jesse studied her face. "You really have never been anywhere but here?"

"Never," Angela said.

"And why would you want to leave a beautiful paradise like this for a wasteland?" Jesse quizzed, but Angela could detect a knowing smile on the corners of his lips. He wanted her to come with him; she could sense it.

"If I can start a life in Chicago and convince my

dad it's safe to leave, then he won't have to sit in a chair in his room reading the same books over and over again, and that won't have to be my fate someday," Angela said. "Besides, we have food here. If there are people in need, maybe I can tell them about this place and help get food to them."

Jesse leaned his body towards Angela. His eyes searched her eyes quizzically, but he said nothing.

"He deserves better than this, and so do I," Angela continued. "I need to find out why he lives like this so I can help him. I need bring him proof that there is a world outside of this garden. To do that, I have to leave."

"So much talk about your father and people in need," Jesse said. He reached out and took her hand in his, causing Angela's heart rate to quicken. "I will take you with me, but only if you want to come with me for yourself. Not for your father or for strangers that you want to save. For you. Are you sure you are ready to leave this all behind?"

Angela hesitated for only a moment before she nodded. "I am."

She heard the smile in his voice when he said, "Then I guess that'll be okay."

THE FOLLOWING NIGHT, ANGELA WAITED IN HER room until her father was asleep. As she lay in bed she could hear the wooden floor creak in her father's adjacent room as he walked from his chair, where he read each night, to his desk, where he kept his books, and then to his bed, where he slept. Once the floor stopped creaking, she listened to him shuffle in bed as he tried to find a comfortable position to rest, but it took him longer than usual to doze off. When all was silent, save for her father's soft snores, Angela placed the biggest backpack she could find on her shoulders and grabbed Jesse's pack from under her bed. She walked over to her window and looked out into the garden. The distance between the windowsill and the world outside seemed wider that night, now that the moment to leave was here. She crept out of her window once again, skillfully climbing down her tree.

In the garden, she put all the fruits she could fit in her packs and filled the few non-cracked bottles they owned with clean water. As she approached the gate, Angela realized she needed to complete one final task. Before she ran away, she wanted to find a safe way to say goodbye to her father. Cursing herself for not doing so before leaving her house, she knew that she would have to go through the front door to get back in. She crept back inside the cabin's kitchen as quietly as a mouse.

As she made her way inside, she realized this was possibly the last time she would be home for awhile, so she found the picture of her mother and put it in her pocket as well. Angela grabbed all of her old newspaper clippings, putting them in her dress pocket. She took the newspaper her father gave her for her most recent birthday and drew a heart on it with the dull remainder of her tiny pencil.

"I'll come back for you," Angela said to herself, placing her tiny pencil onto the kitchen table next to her note. There were butterflies in her stomach from the anticipation of adventure, but these butterflies felt like they had razor blades for wings; like they would eat her alive from the inside out. The pain in her stomach was only second to the pain in her heart.

"I love you," she whispered to herself as she laid the newspaper clipping, her makeshift goodbye letter, on the kitchen table, "but I have to go."

She left quickly, not giving herself an opportunity to change her mind.

ONCE SHE MADE HER WAY BACK OUTSIDE, SHE couldn't help but notice that the air was colder than it was on most summer nights. The wind angrily rattled the leaves of the trees in the garden, as if they knew of Angela's plans to abandon them. The furious feeling the night gave her almost made her think her home was warning her, or that the garden was angry that she would dare leave. Forcing herself forward, she climbed back over the fence to where a sleeping Jesse lay.

"Jesse!" Angela whispered, laying her hand on his shoulder, "Jesse get up!"

Jesse offered a tired smile. When he looked at her, a warm feeling spread through Angela that pushed away the chill. Jesse took his backpack full of food. Reaching his hand into the pack, he pulled out an apple and bit into it.

"You have no idea how good this is compared to what I eat on a daily basis. I haven't had fruit this fresh sense, well, ever," Jesse said. Then, not wanting to appear rude, he offered Angela a bite. She took the apple, sinking her teeth in, then, realizing he needed food more than she did, handed the apple back to him. As they shared their snack, Angela wondered how long the garden's offerings had been his only source of food. It pained her to think that he had been sneaking around and stealing just to eat.

Once the apple was reduced to a core, Jesse stared

at it as if he were contemplating eating it too before finally deciding to toss it onto the ground.

Once Jesse was done with the apple, he reached towards Angela and lifted her arm by her wrist. This startled Angela; she looked into his eyes with confusion.

"Why do you have a broken watch?" he asked.

"It was my mother's," Angela said. "She died when I was a baby."

Jesse looked up at her, compassion in his eyes.

"I'm sorry to hear that," Jesse said. "Do you want me to fix it?"

"If you can," Angela said.

He slipped the object off her wrist and examined it.

"It's not the battery," he mumbled to himself as he fiddled with her watch. Angela waited for a miracle.

Eventually, Jesse was able to get the timepiece to work. Joy built up inside Angela as the hands started to slowly move in a circular fashion. Jesse slid the watch back on her wrist and buckled it tight.

"Good as new," he declared.

"How can I ever thank you?" Angela beamed. "Now, I just need to learn to tell time."

Jesse laughed. "We have our phones for that, right?"

Angela thought about the small black cell phone her father had inside of his room. Like the watch, it didn't work, but Angela didn't feel like confessing that fact to Jesse. They had more important things planned.

"Tonight is the most beautiful night in my entire life," gushed Angela. She tossed back her head and looked at the stars in the sky. "I'm so ready to go to Chicago!"

Jesse smiled back at her. "I am starting to get a little homesick," he admitted.

Angela decided to make small talk to get to know him better. "So . . . what's your favorite fairy tale?" Angela asked.

Jesse looked surprised, then chucked. "I've never given it much thought."

"Really? It's a tie for me," Angela said. "Belle and Rapunzel."

"I was more of a superhero guy myself. Batman's pretty cool," Jesse said.

"You will have to teach me that fairy tale," Angela said. Jesse was silent again. Angela wondered why his eyes looked anxious, almost sad.

"Have you ever wondered what the stars are?" Angela asked, looking up at the sky.

"Burning gas," Jesse answered in a flat tone.

Angela laughed. "No, I'm serious. Do you want to

know what I think?" He nodded. "I think they are moon babies. I don't know for certain, because there are a lot of them. But there was a rabbit in our garden once, a whole healthy rabbit. And it was pregnant! It had a lot of babies. So I assume, over time, it would be possible for the moon to have that many."

Jesse laughed. "I'll suspend my disbelief that you found not one, but two, live rabbits healthy enough to mate, because I'm more curious to learn how the moon manages having babies? Who's the father?"

"Well, I always thought the moon was the father," Angela went on. "The sun is the mother, of course, but she never gets to see them because she is too busy shining in the daytime."

"That's kind of sad, the mother being away and all," Jesse said.

"She can't help it. The moon and the sun are worlds away," Angela explained. "Just because someone's not physically there doesn't mean they are not helping you grow. My mother...I've never met her, but I can feel her. She's somewhere opposite to this, but she's not gone. "

Jesse smiled at her thoughtfully, the hint of anxiety and sadness in his eyes now stronger.

"What's wrong, Jesse?" she asked.

"I love the way your mind works," Jesse finally said; too busy trying to figure out Angela to pay attention to the sky. The wind was chilly. Jesse wrapped his arms around his chest as if giving himself a hug. "Where we are going, life can be a little rough. I want you to know I'll do my best to keep you safe."

"I don't need protecting," Angela said. "Who knows, maybe I'll be the one to keep *you* safe."

Jesse chuckled, "You're so different than anyone I've ever known."

"Oh?" It was all Angela could think to say. She had suspected that she would be very different from people in civilization. This worried her. "Is that bad?"

"No," Jesse assured her. "I like different."

Jesse looked somewhat conflicted. He opened his mouth as if he were about to tell her something important; a warning perhaps, but then changed his mind.

"Tell me about you," Jesse said instead.

"There's not much to tell," Angela said. "I'm sixteen years old and I have done *nothing* with my life."

Jesse smirked. "You make it sound like most sixteen-year-olds have accomplished a lot."

"I assume most have, at the very least, been taught how to read," said Angela.

Jesse said nothing, waiting to learn more.

"I know you want to know about me, but . . . there really isn't much to say," Angela explained cautiously. "I know that I don't want to be stuck here anymore, but I really have no clue what I hope to find once I go. I know that I want to help my father by starting a life in the settlement for us. I think, in order to figure out more, I'll have to leave."

He nodded.

"What about *you?* Your life definitely sounds more exciting than mine," Angela said, trying to take the attention off of herself.

"An exciting life doesn't always mean you are an exciting person," Jesse replied, then sighed. "Angela, I didn't think you would come so late."

"I'm sorry," Angela said. "My dad took *forever* to fall asleep tonight."

"Regardless," Jesse said, "I don't think we should travel right away. If we are going to take off soon, I'm going to need a bit more sleep. How about you stay out here with me tonight so you don't have to sneak back out. Once we get to town, you are going to meet some really exciting people. A lot more exciting than me."

This made the butterflies return to Angela's stomach. She wondered what would it be like to meet other people. Would they all be kind like Jesse, or would the people in the settlement be dangerous? She looked at Jesse, who despite the cold, strong wind, had already dozed off to sleep, and felt comforted by his presence. It would be fine; he would make sure she was okay.

Angela moved closer to Jesse to keep warm. He pulled her even nearer, allowing her to rest her head on his chest, and they fell asleep under the moon and stars.

Chapter Four

Angela was too excited to rest well that night. Fantasies of the journey ahead played in her mind as she drifted in and out of consciousness. At the crack of dawn, she stood up and stretched. Angela wanted to be well on her way before her father noticed her absence, but Jesse was still sleeping peacefully. She used her hand to brush some of his black hair out of his face, causing him to stir and awaken.

"Good morning, sleepyhead," Angela beamed at him.

"Good . . . what?" He said groggily, blinking up at her. Slowly, he pushed himself off the ground and looked around to gain his bearings.

He smiled at her, "Thanks for staying with me last

night. I've been alone for so long, but I liked sleeping next to you."

"Enough sleep," Angela said. "I'm ready to see Chicago."

Jesse frowned at her bare feet. "You really don't have any shoes?" he asked.

"No." Angela was tired of this question. Why must he be *so concerned* with her feet?

"This is going to be a painful journey then," he informed her.

Jesse stood, and Angela realized she may have overestimated his height on the first night she saw him race through her garden . . . he was only a couple of inches taller than Angela's five feet, three inches. He smiled sleepily and took an unfocused step deeper into the forest. As he walked, it took Angela a moment before she realized that he wanted her to follow him. She rushed to catch up.

"How old are you?" Angela asked as they walked.

"Seventeen," he said.

"And the people who live with you in the city; how old are they?" she asked.

"The people of Chicago are various ages, but the people who live with me are mostly older teens and young adults," Jesse said. "Think of us as the anti-Watch. But you might be one of the youngest to join The Resistance."

"I'm not sure I want to meet these Wardens," Angela said.

"They are nothing more than Kane's boy scouts," Jesse explained. "I'd find them amusing if it wasn't for their love of public humiliation and murder."

This caused Angela to freeze in her tracks. She thought of the fates of the outlaws in her father's Wild West novels.

"Are all of the Wardens criminals, then?" Angela asked.

Jesse chuckled, "Depends on who you ask. If you ask one of them, they might say that they are the law."

Jesse turned right, changing the direction they were going in. Angela knew that once they went too far, she would not be able to find her way back home without assistance. This was do or die. She was leaving.

Angela tried to ignore the fact that her feet were tender with blisters. The dry soil was much harder than the dirt in her garden, and she didn't usually have to walk nonstop while at home. Out here, the grass was brown instead of green, and covered in rocks and sticks. Flowers were few and far between. The roots of the trees worked over-time to suck anything out of the dehydrated and poisoned soil. Even the wind was still, a sudden change from last night. The silence around her reminded her of how few animals were left in the forest.

"What's wrong?" Jesse noticed Angela's grim expression.

"I thought the scenery would be prettier," Angela said.

"Surely you didn't think the entire forest looked as magnificent as your garden?" Jesse asked.

Angela shrugged. "A girl can dream."

"Have you ever tried to leave your garden before?" Jesse asked.

"Once," Angela said. "I was six. I didn't get very far."

"I can see why you never tried again," Jesse said. "With a home like that, you have no reason to leave."

"I figured it wasn't safe," Angela said. "My dad warned me about the mutants in the forests."

"There are mutants out here, for sure," Jesse said. "But most are harmless mutated critters.They tend to stay away from people, for the most part."

"Good to know," Angela said.

"It wasn't just the food that kept me around, you know. Your garden is the most beautiful place I've ever seen," he said. "In most places, that type of beauty is a part of history. I'm surprised you came with me so easily."

Angela smiled, "You sound like you were hoping I would come with you this whole time."

Jesse smiled sheepishly, "It's a long journey. Gets a little lonely. I guess I didn't expect to be able to take some of the beauty I found back with me."

Angela chuckled nervously and smiled up at him.

"Well, this settlement is two weeks' walk away right?" Angela asked.

"Yes," he said.

"We have plenty of time. So teach me history," Angela said.

Jesse ran his hand through his hair, brushing it away from the bruise on his face.

"History . . . is a broad topic. What do you want to know?" he asked.

"Can you read?" Angela questioned.

He nodded, and she dug her hand into her dress pocket. She took out all of the old newspaper clippings she had been collecting on her many birthdays. Finally, she would know what they said.

"All I know are fairy tales," Angela said. "Can you tell me these true stories?"

"The line between fact and fiction is shakier than most care to admit," said Jesse.

"What do you mean?" Angela asked.

"I believe that most myths hold a little bit of truth," he said. "Don't dismiss your father's stories."

He took the newspaper clippings and looked them over.

"Oh, these are just random articles. Some of them are about things that happened in other countries," he said, ready to dismiss the topic.

"I don't really understand what a country is," Angela admitted. "Beyond the fact that it's a place." Her father said that when the borders closed during the Bio Wars, people were not allowed to enter or leave the country. Some people were afraid of terrorists getting in and biological warfare increasing. Not long after the war ended, people needed permission to venture beyond their state boundaries as well. She knew there was a lot of talk about keeping track of how many survivors were left in the U.S. and securing borders from threats, but he had never defined a country or a state.

Jesse shrugged, "A country is just a place that adheres to a specific government system. By that definition, I'm not sure if we truly still are one."

He moved on to another newspaper without further explanation, "This one happened in our country. This girl was a survivor of an experimental medical study, and apparently someone kidnapped her a few months before this article was published. This is just reporting that they found her body."

Angela froze in her tracks. The blood drained out of her face, “You mean someone killed her?”

“Killed or drowned, they found her in a lake,” he said. “She most likely was some type of mutant.”

“But why would anyone do that?” Angela asked. She felt like someone was squeezing the air out of her lungs.

“I don’t know, ask the psycho who did it.” He shrugged.

Angela felt a wave of sadness and fear. How could Jesse be so calm about murder? His reaction angered her, and tears gathered in her lashes to spill onto her cheeks.

“Don’t cry. They aren’t all bad,” Jesse’s voice was soft with compassion.

“I’m fine,” she said, hoping she wouldn’t run into any people like that in Chicago. “Read another one.”

“This one is about how twenty percent of people still identify with a religion,” he said. “It’s irrelevant. Religion is outlawed now.”

“What’s a religion?” Angela wanted to learn everything, but was still thinking about the dead child.

“I’m not sure how to explain,” Jesse said, looking at the next newspaper with a grim expression. “It’s something you believe. The people who had them mostly lived before the wars, but I've heard some people still practice in secret. I don't think you need to hear any more of these stories."

"I want to know," she insisted. "I want to learn."

Jesse looked unsure, but did as she asked.

"Well, the next one is an editorial about how racial inequality can impact treatment for mutations," Jesse said.

"What's a race?" Angela asked.

"It's like, your ethnicity? Where your ancestors are from," Jesse explained. "Is the man you live with your biological father?"

"Of course," Angela said. "Why wouldn't he be?"

"You guys aren't the same race, so I was curious."

Angela thought about his question. It had never occurred to her that Nathan could be anything other than her biological father. He had raised her for her entire life.

"I don't understand what you mean," Angela finally said. "If you are talking about why we look so different, I take after my mother. She died when I was a baby, but I've seen photos of her. She was beautiful."

Angela hand instinctively found its way into the pocket of her dress. She clutched her mother's photograph.

"She must have been," Jesse said.

Angela looked Jesse in the eyes, not attempting to hide her nervousness.

"I'm worried that people in Chicago are going to think I'm stupid if I don't learn about all of these things," she confessed.

"They will understand," Jesse assured her. "I mean, it's not like you had a way to get to school, living all the way out here."

Jesse noticed the confusion on Angela's face.

"School?" he asked. "I'm guessing you don't know what a school is."

Angela shook her head.

"Okay, I can't teach you the history of everything, but I can tell you about my life."

Angela learned that Jesse was born in what was once an affluent neighborhood on the outskirts of Chicago, but by the time he was thirteen most of his neighbors' homes were abandoned, so his family moved to the heart of the city. She questioned him about his race and religion and learned he was Asian and Agnostic. He grew up with his parents and his little sister, but had always felt out of step with his family. As a young teenager, he met a girl who told him about a group known as The Resistance. The government viewed this group as a threat because members spoke out against citizenship cards. Jesse told Angela that the penalty for being on American soil without a CitCard was death.

"I don't understand why it would be so important," Angela said.

"There are so few people left in America. They want to keep tabs on us, our purchases, and our locations," Jesse said. "The cards track everything we do. They say it's to keep out terrorists, to rebuild the country. But what Kane wants is control. Without the CitCard, you can't get food or medicine from your settlement's Wardens. Heck, you can legally be killed on sight. They will treat you like you are not human and leave you to die. But not everyone can get citizenship cards, and for the ones who can't, not being carded is a death sentence. The Resistance provides food, shelter, and safety to mutants and others that, for one reason or another, cannot get carded. We are growing in strength and numbers. There are Resistance chapters in other cities. But this movement got its start right here in Chicago. Hopefully, you will decide to help us."

"I would love to help in any way that I can," Angela said, excited to start doing something productive with her life.

Jesse smiled at her offer. "That's what we want to hear."

THAT NIGHT, AS ANGELA LAY ON THE GROUND AND tried to ignore the stones and sticks that clawed at her skin, she heard yowling in the distance. It was an unnatural, shrill sound that rattled her nerves. She looked over at Jesse, who swiftly sat up from where he was sleeping. His hand fell to his waist and pulled out a small black object. Angela gasped when she realized he had been hiding a pistol at his waist.

"Is that a *gun?*" she whispered.

"Wait here," he responded. Before Angela had a chance to reply, he ran off into the wilds.

Each second lasted an eternity as she waited for him to return. She sat still as a board and held her knees to her chest until the crackle of twigs snapping nearby caused her to stand and look around. A jolt of primal fear seized Angela as she saw a large, gray creature moving swiftly towards her. It had characteristics that reminded her of a deer and a fox, with long, skinny legs and a bushy tail. It growled as it charged forward, showing off teeth as sharp as thorns. Its eyes were a blazing red.

Before she could run, she heard the crack of gunfire and a bullet flew past her head. It struck the beast in the skull and the creature shrieked, attempting to retreat before collapsing, blood forming a puddle around it as it died.

Jesse came up behind Angela, enveloping her in his embrace. Angela realized that she had been holding her breath and allowed her lungs to deflate.

"Are you all right?" Jesse asked.

"Of course not!" Angela exclaimed. "You said there were only *critters* in the forest. What type of animal was that?"

"That, like many mutants, are a product of bioengineering. I don't think the government took the time to name all of their new creations," Jesse said. "Come on, we should get out of here before any of its friends show up."

As the pair looked for a safer spot to sleep, Angela realized how little she knew about the war that had destroyed the world. As they set up a new camp, she decided to ask.

"It started the way every horrible thing starts, with good intentions," Jesse said. "Scientists said they were close to unlocking the secrets of immortality and releasing humanity's true potential. They were pioneering a new wave of advanced bioengineering that promised beauty, health, a longer life, and increased intelligence. People signed up in droves. A couple years into the studies, they started doing all kinds of experiments on people who signed up. The most common side effect was death, but others started developing unique abilities. Some of the side effects were straight out of any superhero comic book: increased strength, skin as hot as fire, the whole shabang. These studies were sponsored by the government. I think they wanted to give powerful abilities to soldiers. Other countries saw all the people who died and felt it wasn't humane, rightly so, or maybe they were afraid of facing mutant soldiers, who knows. The first Bio War broke out over it."

"That's awful," Angela said.

"My great-grandfather actually signed up for a study, secretly hoping to end up with a mutation. Crazy guy. Ended up dead, with no powers to speak of," Jesse said. "The people who fought America in that war did so to save the lives of individuals like my great-grandfather."

"I can't believe my father never told me any of that," Angela said. "If all that happened before the war, what happened during it?"

"People don't like to talk about it, so it's hard to get all the details. Much more fun to speak of a time when everyone thought they were about to become Superman," Jesse chuckled to himself. "I do think the government finally realized that enemies make better guinea pigs than citizens. They continued their studies on prisoners of war and started to use biological warfare to poison the enemy's food and water supply and kill them with disease. The rest of the world decided to fight fire with fire. In the first Bio War, the global population was cut in half."

Angela let out a breath. "Well, now I'm adequately depressed."

"Not the fairy tale you were hoping for?" Jesse asked.

"Not at all." Angela shook her head. "It's amazing that after all of that chaos, humanity survived."

Jesse shrugged. "Barely, but yes."

Angela looked down at the watch ticking on her wrist. Something broken had been mended. The tiny object gave her a spark of hope. There was still time to fight for a better world.

OVER THE COURSE OF THEIR JOURNEY, JESSE SHARED more about his life. He talked about the music, movies, and books that he loved. Angela thought her father might like Jesse due to their shared love of Westerns.

Angela learned that he and his friends converted an abandoned warehouse into a home hidden from the Watch's vigilant eye. He was proud of the fact that there was a working television at The Resistance. The world was harsh, and simple pleasures were hard to come by. It took him almost an hour to describe a television to her, because he had to explain how color and light made its way to the screen and how sound found its way out of the speakers.

"Now that I think about it," Jesse said, "there is so much I don't understand about how the technology we used daily actually works. No wonder it's taking what's left of humanity so long to rebuild. It's easier to use the leftovers of yesterday."

They ran out of food a few days sooner than they had projected, but luck seemed to be on their side. On the twelfth day of their journey, Angela woke and realized she had fallen asleep beside a blueberry bush. It had been barren the night before, but berries seemed to grow overnight.

"Wow," Jesse said as they examined the bush, "I guess the soil out here isn't as bad as we thought."

Angela shook her head in disbelief. "I saw that this plant was dead last night! It's almost like it sprouted just for us."

Jesse shrugged. "I've never seen anything like that before. I guess you're my good luck charm."

"Come to think of it," Angela added. "Have you noticed that the grass in our camp is always a little greener when we wake up than it was the night before?"

Jesse chuckled nervously. "Maybe the environment is healing?"

"That would be something," Angela said.

After two weeks, as promised, Angela could see a city skyline in the distance. The decaying skyscrapers were taller than the tallest of trees, but she could tell they were not nearly as grand as they had been in the past. The closer they got to the city, the easier it was to see that the sides of walls were collapsed and few buildings had proper rooftops. Many looked as if someone had been in the process of tearing them down, but stopped halfway through and let the rubble fall over into the streets. There was a finality to approaching this new land; though her mind was full of wonder, her pulse quickened.

Jesse noticed her distress.

"It's okay," he reassured. "You'll be fine. But we are going to have to keep a low profile. You don't have a CitCard yet, so we can't let any Wardens get near you."

"Understood," Angela said.

"We can't just walk in. Let me make a phone call," Jesse said, walking her over to a dirt road in the forest that Angela hadn't noticed before.

Jesse pulled a small, neon-blue object out of his pocket. Angela watched curiously as he poked at it with his fingers and then proceeded to look into the screen and talk. She once found a similar object in her father's box and knew it was a phone, but she had never seen one in use.

"My father said phones don't work anymore," Angela stated. Had her father lied?

"They work locally, inside settlement boundaries," Jesse clarified. "But we can't contact anyone outside our settlements. You wouldn't get any coverage living out there with your father. We are close enough now."

She walked over to stand behind him and peered over his shoulder. There was a tiny face on the screen, moving and talking back to Jesse. Angela could see that it was a woman with blonde hair. Angela moved away and waited for Jesse to finish his conversation.

"Freedom. Hi. Guess who's back?" He laughed and smiled at the phone. "You know I can't stay away from you guys for that long. Pretty sure that Warden forgot about me by now. You're right. Yes, I have a friend with me."

Jesse smiled at Angela. "Freedom is coming."

And for the first time in her life, Angela did not like the sound of freedom. She wanted to apologize for wasting Jesse's time and to go back home, play her piano, and eat soup with her father. It took all her willpower to keep her mouth shut and her feet still.

Chapter Five

A sleek black car drove up the dirt road and parked a few feet away from where Angela and Jesse waited. Angela had never seen a car before. She wondered what propelled its wheels forward and how it knew what direction to go. Realizing she was about to meet another stranger, Angela nervously grabbed onto Jesse's hand. He glanced at Angela and didn't pull away, but his attention was focused on the car.

The door opened and a tall blonde girl emerged. Her black leather boots kicked up dirt on the road as she made her way to where Angela and Jesse waited. Angela recognized her as the girl from the screen. She looked older than Jesse, possibly in her early twenties, and had an athletic build. She wore gray skinny-jeans, a black leather jacket and a black tank top. Sunglasses rested on top of the curly hair that fell down the sides of her shoulders.

The girl glanced at Angela and Jesse's interlocked hands, causing Jesse to take his hand away.

"Oh, crap, he's back again," she said with a smirk.

"Nice to see you again, too," Jesse said. She rolled her eyes at him, but seconds later a smile spread across her face. She pulled him into an embrace.

She turned to Angela, then looked back at Jesse. "What do we have here?"

"Hi, I'm Angela," Angela introduced herself.

"Like an Angel," Freedom said. "How nice. So, what loony bin did Jesse steal you from?"

Angela didn't know how to respond. She looked at Jesse, confused.

"She wants to know where you are from," Jesse said, giving Freedom a stern look.

"I'm not from anywhere," Angela said to Freedom.

Freedom's green eyes glared at her.

"She's not lying. I found her right in the middle of nowhere. But it was a very nice part of nowhere," Jesse stood up for Angela.

"Then how the hell did he convince you to come to this dump?" Freedom asked.

"I want to find a new home for my father and I.

We have lived alone for so long, it would be nice to have some type of community," Angela said.

Freedom stared at Angela's dirty bare feet and messy hair. She turned to Jesse.

"Is she worth the space?" she asked.

Jesse winked. "There is something special about her."

Freedom nodded at Jesse, but Angela could sense that it was not merely a nod of acknowledgment. They were communicating some bit of information that Angela was left in the dark about. Angela looked into Jesse's eyes questioningly.

"Get in the car," Freedom barked at them both. Angela suspiciously walked over to the machine. She touched the car, wondering if it were hot, and realizing it wasn't, she ran her fingers along the outline of the door. She pushed her fingernails between the tiny crack and tried to pry the door open, ignoring the handle. Jesse helped her open the door from inside the car while Freedom watched and laughed.

Jesse slammed Angela's door shut and the car skidded off towards the settlement. Jesse reached over and helped Angela buckle her seatbelt. Angela did not understand why he was strapping her to the car. She started to panic.

"What are you doing?" Angela asked.

"It's to keep you safe in case of an accident,"

Jesse's voice was soft. "Normally I wouldn't bother, not a lot of traffic these days, but I promised to protect you and I will do so in every way I can."

She watched as he strapped himself to the car as well, and decided it must be safe. He showed her the button she needed to click to release the belt when the car stopped.

Freedom watched their exchange thoughtfully from the front seat. Angela noticed Freedom's hands on the wheel, causing the car to turn left or right. So that's how it works, she thought.

Angela looked out of the window and watched the forest float away as they entered an industrial portion of the city. Most of the buildings had patched and boarded windows, the roads themselves were full of craters and debris that caused the vehicle to bounce as they chugged along. At one point, Freedom had to reroute because a sizable portion of a skyscraper was resting in the middle of the road.

"It's incredible," Angela sighed as she looked out of her window.

As they ventured further into Chicago's ruins, Angela could see two other cars bouncing along the mostly empty roads and she spotted a few people travelling by foot.

Angela could hear a soft, melodic sound separate from the roar of the engine. It took her a moment to recognize the unfamiliar instruments and high-pitched voices as music.

"Where is that music coming from?" Angela asked Jesse.

"The car has a radio," Jesse said sleepily. "It plays music."

Freedom laughed, "Boy, Jesse, you really know how to pick 'em."

Jesse's face tightened, but he said nothing. Angela didn't fully understand the implications of her words, but knew it was likely an insult directed at her. She felt a tinge of anger. Why was Freedom being so mean? She was starting to regret coming to Chicago. She was in a strange city, with strange people, and was on her way to meet more people who probably wouldn't like her either. Every inch of her being felt like she didn't belong.

Angela looked out of the window. She had imagined civilization before, but her ideas weren't even close to this reality. For one thing, she didn't expect a settlement this large to be so empty. She had imagined houses like her father's, dozens all together, and one big workhouse where people would make pencils and soap and pianos. In the center of it all would be a palace. She had always pictured a palace. In the fairy tales her father read to her as a child, there had always been one.

Angela knew civilization would not be exactly like her father's stories, with horses and carriages, gladiator arenas, and knights and princes aiming to save damsels in distress. But she expected to at least find the ruins of such a kingdom, instead of the remnants of an alien land. She had not expected to be strapped inside a self-moving cart, rushing past massive, dilapidated buildings. She had not expected that, despite its size, the settlement would feel as bare as the forest surrounding her father's home. Five hundred people in one settlement sounded like a lot to her before, but in a space this vast, she felt lucky whenever she noticed signs of life.

The few people she saw outside her car window did not remind her of her father — still, sure, and calm. They were more like moving pieces of artwork; their clothes, skin, and hair painted in magnificent colors against the grey backdrop of the settlement. Yet, there was a sense of unrest with all of them. She wondered if everyone would be as high-strung as Freedom.

She never saw anyone walking alone; they migrated in pairs or small groups. Her father had always been a keep-to-yourself kind of guy, and Angela expected the rest of the world to be this way too. She wondered if the pairing up was for safety.

Jesse was not even giving his window a glance. He

dozed off, leaving Angela alone with Freedom in the car. Freedom didn't speak again for the remainder of the ride, so neither did Angela.

With Jesse asleep and Freedom silent, Angela found her mind drifting back to her father. She pictured her father waking up and realizing she was missing. It was an image she had been purposely blocking out of her brain for the two weeks she had been traveling. She wondered how he had reacted when he became aware of her disappearance. The reality of what she had done started to settle into her thoughts, and she struggled to keep her worries at bay.

The car found its way to its destination, an old and dilapidated warehouse, and came to a sudden stop.

Chapter Six

As the car came to a full stop, Angela pinched the skin on Jesse's arm to wake him. She tugged and pressed her seat buckle, but was unable to free herself from its clutches.

Jesse jerked his arm away and slowly opened his eyes. Only half conscious, he looked out of the window, then looked back at Angela and smiled.

"Welcome to your new home," he mumbled sleepily.

Angela didn't attempt to mask the worry and disappointment from her eyes. The car had stopped sooner than Angela would have liked.

This building was not tall like the skyscrapers, but it was wide. Boards with stylized letters painted on them covered its broken windows. Angela wondered why this place, of all places, was where Jesse and his friends chose to live. This was not what she expected.

"Come on, Angel," Freedom said, hopping out of the car. She made the word, 'angel,' sound like an insult.

Angela made a show of trying to unbuckle herself in front of Jesse, and he swiftly released her and opened her door. When Angela got out of the car, her bare feet burned as she stood on the hot cement. Freedom walked ahead, unlocking the building's door as Angela and Jesse trailed behind.

The air in the settlement was full of debris and unpleasant smells. The scent inside the building was only a slight improvement. Angela was surprised by the amount of dust that floated through the room, coating the broken furnishings. It did not look as if anyone lived here.

Freedom and Jesse lead her to what they called an "elevator." A yellow paper with handwritten words scrawled upon it was taped to the door. Jesse explained that the sign told outsiders the elevator was in need of repairs. Freedom summoned the elevator with a click of a button. Angela watched in amazement as the doors magically opened without assistance.

"We have no guards, no gate. The best hiding places are right out in the open," Jesse explained as they boarded.

Using the shaky elevator made Angela's stomach queasy. She could hear its bolts rattling as it inched its way down into the unknown. Jesse put his arm around Angela's shoulder until the elevator came to a sudden, shaky stop. The doors crept open and Angela found herself at the end of a long hallway. She could see a dim light shining from around a corner; its source was in another room.

"Have fun, Angel. I've got to go, kids," Freedom said while Jesse walked Angela off the elevator.

"You're not coming?" Jesse sounded genuinely disappointed, which troubled Angela.

"No, I have other business to take care of. I'm sure you'll help her feel right at home." Freedom sent the elevator up as Jesse's face tensed.

"She seems pleasant," Angela said sarcastically, once Freedom was on ground level and out of earshot.

"She's not as bad as she pretends to be," Jesse said. "Come on, there's some people I'd like you to meet."

They walked through the narrow hallway towards the light. Angela could hear laughter and chatter coming from the room. She inhaled deeply and let it out slowly, praying that the butterflies in her stomach would stay still.

Angela peeked into the room before they walked in. It looked clean and modern, therefore out of place in the old dusty building.

Sitting on top of rectangular desks were thin, square devices with illuminated screens. The moving images that danced across them reminded her of the screen on Jesse's phone. A boy sat behind one of them, pressing buttons on a flat device connected to the screens. On one of them, she could see Freedom exiting the elevator. She realized that they were being used to monitor the building. Jesse's prized television sat in the corner, streaming a show.

"Life isn't fair, it's just fairer than death, that's all," one of the women in the room said in unison with the person on the television screen.

Angela was amazed at both the technology and beautiful imagery she saw on the television. Whatever they were watching looked much closer to how Angela had imagined the world to be: a bright green forest and a sky painted blue. The man playfully shoved the shoulders of the woman who had spoken, and they both laughed.

"They are watching *this* crap again?" Jesse groaned.

Angela raised her eyebrow at him.

"You ready?" he asked, reaching out to hold her hand again. Angela offered a slight nod as he squeezed her hand tight. In unison, they stepped into the room.

THE CONVERSATIONS STOPPED AS THREE PAIRS OF curious eyes looked over at Angela. Angela smiled sheepishly at them all.

The first face was attached to a tall woman, older than Jesse, with chestnut-colored skin. She had a nose ring, blue fingernail polish, tightly coiled hair, and brown eyes. She was wearing jeans and a black t-shirt that showed an image of four men playing musical instruments. She had been the one quoting the television. Jesse said the woman's name was Rain and that she was their resident medic.

The second face belonged to a male in his early twenties. He wore a blue t-shirt and denim shorts and his skin was extremely pale, whiter than both Jesse's golden tone and her father's fair skin. He was taller than Jesse and his hair was so black it was almost blue. His slim face and wide eyes stared blankly at Angela until he finally twisted it into a crooked smile.

He was the one who had playfully poked Rain. Jesse told Angela that his name was Zinc and that he was a coder.

The last face belonged to a petite teen girl in an off-white sundress. Angela figured the girl was at least fifteen, but she could pass as much younger. She had olive skin, large brown eyes, and a heart-shaped face. Her most noticeable feature was her bright blue hair that fell just below her shoulders, and the soft pink ribbon she was using as a headband. Angela learned that this girl was named Emi and that she was a recruiter.

Emi was the first of the three strangers to approach Angela, which she did by running over and giving her a warm hug. Angela, surprised at the sudden show of affection, whispered a barely audible, "Hello."

"It's so nice to have new people on the team!" Emi greeted.

"Jesse, next time you better bring us a cute guy back, okay?" Rain told Jesse, giving Angela a small smile.

"I'm already here, baby," Zinc said with a goofy grin, before turning back to his computer screen.

"Please." Rain rolled her eyes.

"So, what's your name and where are you from?"

Emi inquired. She was still peering up at Angela with a huge grin on her face.

"Angela. And I'm more interested in where I'm going."

"You like adventure then?" Emi asked.

"I'm not sure, yet," Angela admitted. "But I know that I would like a better life. If that entails adventure, so be it." She was surprised that no one had said anything about her messy appearance yet.

"Well good, because we need *all* the help we can get," Emi stated. "May I ask why you decided to follow Jesse back to Chicago?"

"I want to find a happy ending, for my father and I," Angela said. "And, I suppose, for the rest of the world as well."

"That's what she thinks," said Jesse. "But I think she already had a pretty happy life, and grew bored of it."

"I was a little bored," Angela admitted. "But you can't have a happy ending without first reading the full story, and I've never even been taught how to read."

Emi eyes widened, "Really? That's a shame. We have quite the library here. We have collected six books."

Angela laughed. "Just six? You should meet my father."

"Look, Angela," Rain spoke up. "It's great that you want to help us, but you are looking a little rough. I know it's been a long trip, do you want to wash up?"

A bath sounded like heaven to Angela, and she eagerly nodded as Rain beckoned her to follow.

Chapter Seven

Even after Rain explained how the shower worked and taught Angela how to turn on the water, it still fascinated her. There was no fire to boil the water that streamed from the metal tube that hung over the bathtub. Angela wondered how the water became warm. Closing her eyes and enjoying the feeling of the water hitting her tired skin, she decided it didn't matter. There were many strange things about this settlement, and she knew she would not figure them all out in one day. She washed her hair, relieving it of the dirt from the forest and causing it to curl into tiny ringlets; then her face, letting the white bubbles float down her body.

After she was done, she wrapped a blue cotton

towel around her body, stepped out of the tub and walked over to the clothes left out for her.

The clothes belonged to Rain, who was five foot eight and had longer legs than Angela. Angela hadn't worn pants since she was a toddler. Dresses were more comfortable and easier to make. Rain's pants bunched up at the bottom and were baggy on Angela's slim hips. The shirt, a blue cotton tank top, left her arms and shoulders exposed. She frowned at her reflection in the bathroom mirror as she slid red flip-flop sandals onto her sore feet.

Angela walked out of the bathroom and went back to the surveillance room. Everyone stopped their conversations when she entered. Rain stared at her critically. Zinc's head peered over his computer screen to look her over, and a small, amused smile crept across his face. Emi looked sympathetic.

"Aw, you poor girl. We have to go get you some clothes," Emi said.

"You can't go anywhere with her right now. She's not even carded, yet," Jesse interjected.

"Do I really need to be carded?" Angela spoke up. "Didn't you say that was a bad thing?"

"Not all laws are good things, we still gotta follow them," Jesse answered. "Don't worry, we have come up with a way for you to be safely carded without the Watch actually knowing your every move. Think of it as your first fake ID, only you still can't get into any bars."

Angela did not know what a bar was, but figured this was supposed to be a joke because everyone around her giggled. She forced a small laugh that lasted a little too long.

After a moment of silence, she spoke up again, "How do you make this fake ID?"

"All of our equipment is below," said Jesse. Angela wondered it he were attempting another joke.

"But...we are below," Angela said, remembering that the elevator had descended below ground level. "Aren't we?"

Jesse walked to the corner of the room and got onto his knees. He pulled back the edge of the large rug that covered most of the floor, revealing what looked like the faint outline of a square door built into the ground. Jesse pushed it down. Dust flew into the room as it swung open, revealing a small crawl space, hardly big enough for two people in width, but deeper than it was wide. Inside this space was another door. Jesse got inside and unlocked it to reveal a dark tunnel.

"Of the building, yes; of the settlement? No." Jesse said.

"And you thought my garden was interesting,"

Angela said. "You literally have a basement under your basement!"

"It's a little bit more involved than that. You'll have to follow me to find out," Jesse said, pulling a flashlight out of his pocket and leading the way.

Angela jumped into the tiny space and walked into the smelly tunnel. The odor was even worse than outside. Even with the flashlight on, she could hardly see anything other than the tunnel's dark walls. She could not make out how long the tunnel was or what they were approaching.

"Welcome to The City Below," said Jesse.

He explained that under Chicago, there were the remnants of tunnels used in a large train system that was once called "the L." Most of the entrances to the train system had been locked down. In addition to the subway train systems, there were networks of other tunnels that ran underground. There were pathways once used by old abandoned freight trains and cable cars, and new tunnels created by citizens during the Bio Wars to hide mutants. Some spaces were smaller than a hallway, and meant to hide people underneath a house; others were huge and interconnected. Those who were in the know enough to find an entrance, collectively knew all of these tunnel systems as The City Below.

Jesse told Angela that some people spent their

entire life underground, while many people who live above ground thought The City Below was a myth. It was still mostly mutants who used The City Below, but it also housed bandits and outlaws who wanted to trade, kill, or simply live in private. It was a safe haven for people who didn't have any options above ground.

"That makes me feel so safe," Angela said sarcastically. "I saw firsthand how dangerous the mutants can be on our way to the city."

"Some are dangerous. Some are not. But most of the murders that happen in Chicago are due to the Watch, not mutants," Jesse explained.

"Are they down here?" Angela asked. "The Watch?"

"During the war, the authorities used to raid The City Below to kill off mutants who took refuge. They also hunted and killed runaway mutants in the forest. These days, the Watch seems to be focusing their efforts on the settlement above ground. I think they figure once you are living off the grid in a world like this, you are as good as dead."

Jesse said she had little cause to worry about the Watch or mutants, as the tunnel they had entered was separated from the remainder of The City Below and had been securely blocked off. The only way in was through The Resistance headquarters. There was a door inside this tunnel that lead to the larger City Below, and he had the key. He kept it in case they ever needed to go through The City Below to exit Chicago. The larger tunnel housed many mutants and outlaws, but the area they were in was safe. The only entrance to this section of it was at The Resistance.

She followed Jesse to a door and watched as he opened the room with a key. He said that the room was once used as a large storage unit.

This room had light even though the rest of the tunnel was in complete darkness. Jesse told Angela that The Resistance used something called a power generator to create light underground. She could hear the hum of the machine powering the room.

As she looked around the room, the first thing that caught her eye was a tiny greenhouse growing a small amount of food under a bright light. It looked pitiful compared to the plentiful food available in her garden back home, but it was still nice to see green in such a gray, concrete city.

There were black, metal objects hanging from the walls that were so foreign to Angela she almost dismissed them as decorative. It took Angela a moment to realize they were guns, having never seen such weapons before. They were bigger than her father's or Jesse's pistol, rivaling the rifle's on the cover of her father's Wild West books. In addition to the guns, there were large swords and knives from the worst parts of her favorite fairy tales. Angela examined them, imagining one was Excalibur and she would soon be preparing for a dangerous quest.

Cabinets lined the walls, and two large desks with machines on them took up a considerable portion of the room's space. Jesse told her that these machines and the machines she saw upstairs were called computers. Next to one computer was a desk with camera on it.

In the corner, so still and silent that Angela hadn't noticed them right away, four people sat in the room. They watched Angela intently. Angela was shocked to see that one of the people, a man who looked like he couldn't be older than 30, was locked inside of a cage. He appeared a bit delirious, yet he smiled at Angela.

"Why is that man locked up?" Angela whispered, feeling uneasy again. Jesse shut the door behind Angela, locking it with his key. There was little she could do to stop Jesse from putting *her* in a cage if he so desired. Following him down here may have not been her brightest moment.

"Jesse," she repeated, "what's going on down here?"

"Better locked away than dead," said Jesse. "He looks like you and I, but he has mutated. It's a simple mutation: That man's blood and sweat have become extremely acidic; touching his blood could burn our skin. To the Watch, that's reason enough to kill him. His family came to us for help, yet his condition has proven very difficult to cure. He is also a bit delirious, and becomes violent sometimes. As we work to find a cure, we can't let him touch our other guests, lest he harm his children."

The other "guests" included a woman with a young girl, about five, and a slightly older boy, about seven. Jesse told her the woman's was named Becca, the caged father was Julian, and the young boy and girl were Lucas and Maria. Becca looked weary, but the children smiled at Angela and Jesse.

"Hello," Angela said to the family. After a long pause, Lucas spoke up.

"Are you . . . like daddy?" he asked.

Angela looked at Becca for answers, not understanding the question.

"She can't speak English," Jesse explained, "but the little ones can."

"What does he mean by 'like daddy?'" Angela asked.

"He wants to know if you will be staying here, if you have mutations in your blood that we need to treat as well," Jesse said, before turning to the boy.

"No, I'm afraid the pretty girl will be staying upstairs with me," Jesse winked at the child before turning back to Angela. "This family . . . none of them are carded. We provide a safe space for them, food and shelter. But no one wants to live in a cage their whole life. One day, we hope to be part of the cause that allows men like Julian to see the light of day again without being killed for it. To hold his children again without causing them harm. If you wanted to know what The Resistance is all about, take a look around you."

Angela frowned. Despite his seemingly noble reasoning, she could not wrap her head around the fact the Jesse felt it was okay to keep a family locked up in this room.

"If you can make fake CitCard for me, why can't you make fake cards for all of the mutants?" Angela asked.

"If too many people have fake cards the Watch will become aware and crack down on it. The cards will be useless," Jesse said. "Besides, we cannot give someone who has obvious mutations a fake card. It won't do them any good as it will just get revoked and they will still be killed."

"But can't they stay upstairs, at least the mom and kids?" Angela asked, her eyes focusing on the weapons again.

"They are a family," said Jesse. "They want to stick together. Sometimes being separated from those you love is more of a cage than any room can be."

Suddenly Angela felt guilty for leaving her father. At least her cage was much nicer than this.

Angela nodded in agreement, but she was still unsure how she felt about the whole thing. This room, with the huge guns and sharp swords hanging from the walls, was no place for children to grow up. He did say The Resistance was the "anti-Watch," but she didn't know how literal they took their role. Jesse said that the Watch were killers, but with so many weapons, were The Resistance killers too?

"What are the guns for?" Angela asked.

"Mostly just protection," Jesse said. "Just practicing our Second Amendment rights that the Watch seems to think is only for them."

"Mostly?" Angela questioned. "Have you . . . used a gun?"

"Many times," said Jesse.

"Have you ever killed anyone?" Angela asked.

Angela's heart sank when Jesse didn't answer right away.

"I would never kill in cold blood, like the Wardens do," he finally said, "I have only killed once. I received an assignment to kill a Warden after he murdered a member of The Resistance."

"Then you're just as bad as them," Angela said.

"Easy to say when it's not your family being murdered," Jesse said. "The people of The Resistance, they are my family. If someone ever harmed your father, what would you do?"

Angela ignored his question.

"Was that why you ran away to the forest?" Angela asked, " Because you killed a Warden?"

"Yes. But that Warden had killed thirty-nine innocents, including my best friend, and was on his way to publicly execute three more. When Freedom offered me the assignment, I saw it as a way to prevent more deaths. Three people lived because of my choice. Having to lay low afterward turned into a good thing, because I got to meet you."

Angela said nothing. If Freedom ever asked her to kill someone, no matter who they were or whatever reason she gave, Angela knew she couldn't. It wasn't in her to take the life of another.

"Don't worry, Angela," Jesse said. "I did not bring you here to turn you into a killer. Other than Freedom, Emi, and I, no one else here has ever touched a gun. You will not have to use one. I said I would protect you and you are safe with me."

They walked over to an area of the room with a green screen. He told her to stand in front of the screen and smile. Angela beamed at the camera, and he told her that smiling was only allowed if she did not show her teeth. Her toothless smile felt fake. The camera flashed, which startled Angela. Jesse uploaded the picture onto one of the computers.

"Now remember, the credits on this card are fraudulent and should only be used in an emergency or to buy needed items," Jesse said. "We want to stay under the radar."

The counterfeit CitCard emerged from a nearby printer, and Angela looked the card over before putting it in her pocket. She could not read the name on the card, so she turned to Jesse.

"What's my alias?" Angela asked.

To her surprise, he had used her real first name. Angela's new last name was Woods, which Jesse said he selected due to her former residence. Angela realized she didn't know her father's last name and had never thought to ask. Even though the guns and cage disturbed Angela, she smiled at the fact that she now had a last name.

"The Watch aren't very good at distinguishing real CitCard's from fake cards. Still, Kane has given them permission to kill un-carded individuals with no trial, so it's best to avoid situations where you have to actually show them the card."

"Trust me. I have no desire to get anywhere near the Watch," Angela said.

Angela said goodbye to the children and waved at

the mother and father before she and Jesse made their way back to the abandoned building, where Emi was waiting patiently.

"I want to take you shopping with me, Angela!" Emi gushed excitedly as soon as Angela made it back.

Angela was nervous about going outside and blending into this new world. Still, she knew she needed some clothes and shoes if she wanted to avoid being spotted as an obvious outsider.

"That would be great," Angela said. "Let's go."

Chapter Eight

The market was located inside of a large mall once known as *Water Tower Place.* Despite the dreary ambiance that shrouded the rest of the settlement, this location was busy and bright. All of the mall's official storefronts were vacant, but various vendors lined the halls, selling their wares to make a buck and playing music from radios or their own instruments to pass the time. Others gathered around an old fountain that no longer worked, trading personal items and food with other visitors.

A Warden manned the most frequented stand. He didn't look like the ruthless killers Jesse had made the Watch out to be. He was a short, round, middle-aged man who reminded Angela of her father. He wore black pants and a shirt with red, white, and blue stripes, reminiscent of the American flag that her father had at home, only with one large copper star on his chest instead of stars representing each state. Emi said the star was something that Kane added to his version of the American flag, symbolizing the rebirth of America. He was drawing the biggest crowd of customers, selling the most food and supplies to the shoppers. Two other Wardens guarded the entrance of the mall, but these were slim and fit.

"I have a question to ask, Angela," Emi said as they explored the market, looking for a vendor selling clothing.

"What's that?" Angela was only half paying attention. There was so much to see. The architecture alone made Angela less impressed by her father's ability to build their cabin.

Emi slowed her walking pace down a little bit. An embarrassed smile spread across her face.

"I'm nosy," Emi admitted. "You don't have to answer if you don't want to, but do you like Jesse?"

"Of course I like him." Angela didn't understand the implications of her question. "He's been very kind to me."

"Yes, yes, Jesse is very kind. But do you like him, like him. I hope so, maybe he'll get over his little crush on Freedom. That would be so fire!" Emi jumped up and down with excitement. "And it's so obvious he likes you. You two would make such a cute couple."

Angela realized that Emi was talking about "liking" in a romantic way. The way she had heard about in stories. The way her father once loved her mother.

"Oh, well, I don't really know if I like him in that way. Maybe I do, I don't know yet," she clarified. A few weeks ago, she didn't know any other humans existed. It was too much of a mental leap to contemplate romance with one of them so soon. *Especially* one who had just confessed that he had killed a man.

"Well, if you figure it out, let me know. I love to play Cupid," Emi said, before latching on to Angela's arm and guiding her to a vendor.

"You'll be the first to know," Angela promised, wondering who Cupid was.

It was easy being around Emi. She was energetic and positive, yet patient with Angela, understanding that everything about the settlement was new to her. For the first time since arriving in Chicago, Angela started to relax.

The clothing that the vendor was selling was made in a variety of bold colors instead of the bland, repurposed fabrics she used to sew with back home. Most of the clothes were used, but the vendor said that some items were hand made and brand new.

They purchased three shirts, two pairs of pants, and

two dresses. Though Angela was happy to find clothing that fit, she was more interested in the electronic items she had seen another woman selling in the mall. After they made their purchases, she dragged Emi to a vendor that had a cardboard sign with the word, "Unplugged" written on it in blue stylized print. Four cell phones sat on a threadbare blanket in front of the woman.

The vendor, a pretty twenty-something with dozens of braids atop her head, had a nametag on her red shirt that said her name was Stella and that she was a "Sales Manager." Emi snorted at the formal title.

"Pretentious much?" Emi mumbled to herself.

Emi seemed unenthused as the woman showed her wares, but Angela was awestruck. The phones all had unique abilities. It seemed that at the end of the world, people were willing to invest in staying connected.

"This one's the Microplay. It was the last phone made before the Bio Wars, but Kane's team has updated it. The coolest thing about it is that it connects to your CitCard and you can wirelessly communicate in any way with the entire world," Stella said, her voice high pitched and bubbly. "You can talk to anyone in the city, buy anything from anywhere. It learns your taste and updates you on the latest things you may like. You can ask it anything and it will find the answer."

"If it buys things you don't need, it sounds like a waste of money," Emi said.

"Anything?" Angela was astonished.

"Go ahead, ask it anything." Stella looked smug.

"What's my name?" Angela talked to the phone. A woman's face appeared on the screen. Emi looked slightly terrified.

"Angela," the smiling face said in a conversational tone. Emi heaved a sigh of relief, as if she expected something far worse to happen.

"Wow!" Angela exclaimed.

"It's beautiful, isn't it? You can even ask it questions about other people's cards. Next time you see a cute boy walking down the street, you can ask your phone if he's single." She giggled.

Angela looked up at her, confused. "How would the card know that?"

"Cards keep track of things like that. The technology is fascinating," she said.

Angela nodded. Despite the war's effects on the economy and population, the technology in Chicago still was far beyond anything she had ever imagined. She figured most of these items must have been invented before the Bio Wars.

"It's on sale, only nine hundred credits," Stella offered.

"We were just looking today, but thanks," Emi spoke up, grabbing Angela's hand and pulling her away before she could be sucked into another item. Emi whispered that buying anything that expensive would draw attention to their counterfeit cards.

In the distance, Angela saw a man in a bright yellow suit pulling a large cage atop wheels through the mall. The cage had a curtain draped over it to hide what was inside. A crowd was gathering around the man.

"Step right up, step right up!" the man yelled through the mall. "Come see a real, live post-human for yourself! Right in this here cage! On his way to his execution!"

Emi grimaced. "Bounty hunters make me sick."

A crowd of about fifteen people started to gather around the man, including a couple of vendors who left their stands to see the spectacle. The cage was partially eclipsed by the black curtain, so that viewers would have to pay the man in order to see what was inside.

"Post-human," Angela said. "What's a post-human?"

"In the war, we were attacked by biological

weapons, drugs, and poisons," said Emi. "Some people died, but others simply . . . changed. Post-human is just another word for people with mutations, while mutant is a more general term that can also be used for animals. Most post-humans were killed or experimented on during the war, some retreated away from civilization to live out their last days in peace. Some still live in the forest, most hide in The City Below."

"Like Julian," Angela said, remembering the man in the tunnels below The Resistance.

Angela approached the booth and tried to see through the crowd. Emi warned her not to pay any money, but underneath the curtain Angela could see what looked like large, hairy feet in shackles. She could hear the creature's distressed groan, its voice echoing through the mostly empty mall. Was this what her father described as a monster? She had never really thought about the fact that they were once human.

"Not all post-humans look like monsters, others still look like you and I, but have unique abilities or immunities from drugs or radiation. The monstrous-looking ones were often killed on sight, but it's possible to have a gift that goes undetected," explained Emi. "This one is more of a monstrous sort."

"The man that captured him doesn't look like a Warden," Angela said.

"He's probably a bounty hunter," Emi explained. "They go into The City Below and catch mutants to sell to the Watch."

Angle listened to the low howl that escaped the creature's lips. It was hard to imagine that this being was once human.

"Come on, we have to go," said Emi, pulling Angela away from the creature, out of the mall, and back onto the settlement streets. Outside the mall, three Wardens stood at attention, their guns ready to fire.

"Oh crap," Emi said. "I didn't realize an execution was scheduled for today."

Angela stepped back, closer to the market door, as other shoppers pushed past her to step outside. Her heart pounded so loud she worried the Wardens could hear it beat, but the guns were not pointing towards her.

The guns were pointed at the head of a girl who looked all of twelve years old. The child's hands were bound together by a metal cuffs. She sat on her knees and cried for mercy.

"Please," her voice was raspy and her breathing heavy. Strands of yellow hair and sweat clung to her face. "I would never use . . . my gifts . . . against anyone. Please, I could be of service to you."

The Wardens were not fazed. One even laughed as they fired at the child in unison. The girl fell to the ground. Emi grabbed Angela and tried to turn her away from the scene, but it was too late. Angela has seen the red blood flow onto the concrete as the men tasked with feeding and watching over the settlement killed the child in cold blood. She screamed as Emi pulled her away from the crowd.

"I'm so sorry you had to see that . . . I'm so sorry," Emi said as they made their way back home. "They kill them in public to make a spectacle out of it. They are trying to show their power."

"She was just a little girl," said Angela, tears building up in her eyes. "Why would they hurt a child?"

"She's not a child to them," Emi explained. "She's a mutant."

When Angela's father had spoken to her about mutants, the image she had in her mind was akin to the beast in the forest. What could be so dangerous about a child that warranted her death?

The doors to the mall opened and the man pushed the cart carrying the second mutant to the Wardens. The creature continued to whimper and howl as the cart bounced over cracks in the concrete. The Wardens offered the man a small bag containing some type of payment for his good deed of capturing the poor creature. The Watch readied, and the three raised their guns again, in unison. By this time, everyone inside the mall had come out to watch. Some of the onlookers were silent, but many cheered the Warden's on. Emi rushed Angela far away from the crowd. As Angela shut her eyes tightly and tried to block out the world, she heard the distant gunshots go off and the creature's final plea of distress.

Chapter Nine

Emi felt it wasn't safe to stay out with so many Wardens hyped up following an execution, so after the shopping trip she took Angela straight back to The Resistance. This was fine by Angela. After seeing two mutants executed, one right in front of her eyes, Angela had no desire to ever step foot outside again. No wonder the family below was okay with living underground. She understood why Jesse keep them there, now that she saw death was their only other option. Wanting to rid herself of Rain's oversized clothing, Angela went to her room to change, trying to block out the images of the young girl's death or the sound of the creature's pleas.

Angela sat on her bed and reminded herself why

she had come to the settlement: to build a better life for her and her father. She pushed her thoughts about the Wardens and their victims to the back of her mind and started trying on her new things.

She promised herself that when she went to get her father, she would bring gifts from the settlement: clothing, unique foods, and new books for him to read. Maybe this would encourage him to venture out and join her in Chicago. They were not mutants, so they could get real CitCards and not be in any danger from the Watch. Instead, the Watch would sell them food and medicine and allow them to live relatively safe lives. However, it would be difficult to turn a blind eye on the plight of the mutants after what she had witnessed. Angela slipped on a baby blue dress and headed down the hall to give Rain her clothes back.

The Resistance headquarters had many rooms. Beyond the main room with the surveillance cameras, computers, and the hidden passage to The City Below, there was a hall that led to eight other tiny rooms. Angela opened door after door before she found Rain's room. Rain was perched on her bed, bobbing her head to a tune on the radio.

"Thanks again for letting me borrow your clothes," Angela said shyly, putting the clothing on her desk.

"No problem," Rain gave Angela a small smile. "Did you enjoy the market?"

Angela hesitated. "The market was nice. Wasn't expecting the execution that took place outside of it."

Rain's eyes grew wide. "Oh, I'm sorry you had to see that!"

Angela sighed, "I'm starting to understand why my father didn't want me to leave."

Angela looked around the room. Movie and band posters fully covered her walls, and an old photograph sat next to her bed. Angela saw a younger Rain grinning ear to ear. Next to her was an even younger girl, around age eight, giving the camera a cheeky grin that showed off the fact that one of her front teeth were missing. Angela decided that while she was here, she might as well try to make friends.

"Where is she, the girl in the picture?" Angela asked.

"Dead," Rain said, "same as my parents."

"I - I'm sorry," Angela said.

"It's fine," said Rain. "It is what it is. We all caught the same disease. I was the only survivor."

"Did The Resistance cure you?" Angela asked.

"No," Rain said. "I cured me, and then The Resistance recruited me to help cure others. I only wish I could have saved my family as well."

Angela wanted to change the subject.

"So was all this music made before the war?" Angela asked, pointing to the radio that was sitting on the desk. She didn't know if people were making new things or using the old world's leftovers like her father.

"Biological weapons can't kill the radio. I'm certain our data will outlive us," Rain explained as she turned the radio on. "These were pre-war, but I'm sure some people are still making music as a hobby. Tragedy begets art. Do you like my music?"

The music switched from a song with loud instrumentals and a near-screaming vocalist to one with a pounding bass and fast words.

"It's very . . . loud," Angela said.

"Well, what type of music do you like?" Rain asked.

Angela considered her question. It was only recently that she realized music came in different "types," and now she was expected to know these types by name.

"The piano," Angela decided.

Rain's eyes got wider. "A classic! Fire! I have them on my MP3."

She got up and switched the radio to another screaming vocalist.

"If everything was perfect, we'd have no control," Rain sang quietly to herself while the vocalist screamed. Rain looked at Angela expectantly, singing, *"But it's gonna take some time, to turn off the common sense in my mind."*

Angela stared at Rain blankly, feeling slightly uncomfortable.

"It's almost like this world is for show, it's pretty outside, and there's nowhere to go, in this vast nation, stuck in my imagination." Rain's eyes were still locked on Angela, hoping to get a reaction from her. *"I don't know what to say, because these things won't go away."*

"That's not a piano," Angela finally said.

"Oh . . . I thought you meant the band, *Piano Poltergeist*." Rain paused her radio. "You really are from the middle of nowhere, aren't you?"

Angela suddenly felt embarrassed. There was too much to get caught up on. She missed home where life was simple and she was seen as competent. Or did her father think she was stupid all along? She thanked Rain for the clothes again and said she needed to get going. She exited the room without saying another word.

Rushing out the door, she bumped into Jesse. Had he been waiting outside, listening to her embarrass herself?

"Whoa," Jesse grinned at her. "You act like you're running from a ghost."

Angela felt butterflies in her stomach, but this time they were different, less vicious. The razorblades had disappeared. Even though she still felt embarrassed from her encounter with Rain, she didn't have much control over the smile that appeared on her face.

"Jesse!" she all but cheered. "I missed you."

Jesse chucked, surprised at her enthusiasm. "I missed you too," he said. He held her hand and gave it a small, reassuring squeeze.

"Come with me," Jesse continued. "I want to tell you more about what we do."

He pulled her towards the elevator.

"Wait," said Angela. "I'm not sure I want to go back out there."

Jesse's eyes softened. "Emi told me what happened. I promise, I won't let you near any Wardens."

Sheepishly, Angela nodded. "Okay."

Why was it so much easier to be around him that anyone else in this place? They got back on the scary elevator and exited the abandoned building. This time, since Angela had taken a shower and was wearing her fancy new used shoes; she blended in with everyone else in town.

Angela was unsure about being outside at night after seeing what the Watch were willing to do in the middle of the day, but even after elaborating on what she had witnessed, he didn't seem concerned.

"That's exactly why I want to take you out at night, to show you how to stay safe in the settlement," he explained. Angela was still apprehensive, but being with Jesse was comforting. Jesse wanted to make sure she knew the lay of the land, so they walked for hours, careful to avoid the Watch.

As they ventured across the city, he made sure Angela knew her limitations. To get into any of the Watch's guarded buildings in the city, she would need a real CitCard. He pointed out the buildings where her fake card would not be good enough and showed her safe places to buy food and supplies, such as the homes of independent farmers and craftsmen, places where her card's money credits were unlikely to be detected as counterfeit. Angela wasn't very interested in getting inside the forbidden buildings. She wanted to talk to Jesse about uniting her two worlds.

"I was wondering when we could go back home and bring my dad here?" Angela interrupted as they walked down an empty sidewalk. "It would do him good to live with other people."

"Soon enough," said Jesse.

"How soon? I know he's worried sick about me,"

Angela said. "Don't get me wrong, I love being here with you and I don't think it could have happened any other way, but I do feel bad about the way I ran off. If I go back now, I will have proof that people are alive out here. He will see that it's safe to leave home and we can both be part of this community."

"We risk a lot when we go in and out of the settlement," Jesse said. "The only reason Freedom let me leave before was because I had killed a Warden and needed to hide. She also had a private mission she wanted me to look into."

"What was the mission?" Angela asked.

"It's called a private mission for a reason," Jesse said. "The point is, I think Freedom will be more likely to let you leave the settlement again after you have some work under your belt. Let her see what you can contribute to our community, and she will let you bring your father to stay with us."

They walked and talked until the late night turned to early morning and then they sat and watched the sun rise above the broken skyscrapers. He told her he wanted her to experience classic Chicago, so they trekked all the way to a place he called Navy Pier, an old amusement park that still held the ruins of its rides. As they approached, Angela's heart started to pound as a large body of water came into view.

"It's the ocean!" she declared, grabbing Jesse's wrist and pulling him away from the Pier and closer to a small beach. She slipped off her shoes, allowing her feet to sink into the sand as cool waves washed over her toes.

"Not exactly," said Jesse. "But it's the best we've got."

Angela wiggled her toes in the sand as cool water splashed her ankles.

"Careful there," Jesse said. "There are toxins in the water. If you have any type of cut on your skin, you could get really ill. Even without any open wounds, most people don't risk it."

"Oh, right," Angela moved her feet out of the water. She pulled the picture of her mother out from her pocket and showed it to Jesse.

"She was here," Angela said. "My mother was in Chicago."

Jesse examined the photo, "Sure looks like it. I know Lake Michigan when I see it."

"This must have been the city I was born in, before my mother died and my father hid me away," Angela said. "I just don't understand why he left! Do you think he was un-carded? But *why* did he tell me there was no one else alive? There is a whole world out here."

There was compassion in Jesse's eyes. "My guess would be to keep you there."

Angela's eyes met Jesse's. "*Why?* Do you really think he was not my biological father? Do you think he kidnapped me and took me away, or something?"

"I never said that," Jesse said. He attempted to change the subject, taking her hand and pulling her away from the beach.

"Navy Pier is just over here. I want to show you the Ferris wheel," Jesse pointed at the giant metal circle that stood over 150 feet against the sky. "It still works. There's a family who has a party out here every Halloween. They always bribe the settlement Wardens to turn this one ride back on, and everyone gets on and goes around. Did you know that the first Ferris wheel ever made was built right here in Chicago?"

"Turn it on?" Angela asked. "What does it do when it's on?"

"The karts go up to the top, you can see the whole settlement. If you stick around, maybe I can show you someday. It's the best view you could ever imagine," Jesse said.

Angela looked up at him defiantly. "Why not today?"

"Well, I'm not in any position to try and bribe the

Watch," he said. "Besides, we need to get going. It's time to head back home."

THE SUN WAS STARTING TO RISE OVER THE settlement. Jesse took Angela through Millennium Park on their way back. Angela enjoyed seeing her reflection as she walked under an enormous mirrored sculpture Jesse called "the Bean." A few other people were in the park: a father and child playing tag and a man putting various trinkets on a blanket to sell them to passers-by. Angela took in the man's hair, bright green, and his face, covered in tattoos.

"When more of your freedom is getting taken away, the more you want to feel like an individual. A lot of people are turning into mod-freaks," Jesse said. "People have been getting more tattoos, piercings, and skin treatments than ever. The new popular ones are eye-color changes, eye tattoos, and skin-color changes. It's a visual way to flaunt your money, if you happen to still have any. The lead singer of Piano has fake, bright red skin. Rain likes it, but I think he looks like he has a permanent sunburn."

Angela laughed, "But how could they possibly do that?"

"If you have money, you can pretty much do

anything," Jesse explained. "Did you know that before the war, scientists figured out how to slow down aging? The oldest man lived to be 201 years of age. But no one has money for things like that anymore. But, tattoos . . . tattoos are something that today's rich can afford."

"Doesn't everyone get the same amount of credits from the Watch?" Angela asked.

"Yes, everyone gets an equal amount of rations from Kane, but we still buy and sell to each other. Some people are better equipped to earn more credits on their own. The rich have goods and resources that help them make extra money."

Angela tried to imagine what it meant to be rich in a world with so little, but she had no point of reference.

"How do you become rich?" Angela asked.

"If I knew that, I would be rich," Jesse laughed. "It's old money mostly. You needed money to survive the war, to buy food and try experimental medicines. Then, you needed money to buy cures when those drugs did not work. Today's middle class is yesterday's well off. The one positive thing that came out of this is it has taught people to be more cooperative. Back then, people thought their money would keep them safe, and many opted to live alone rather than in community with others. After the war, the survivors all migrated back to these large settlements to help each other out. We found that we need each other to stay alive and share resources. If you think about it, it is kind of beautiful that for humanity's survival, we have no other option than to stick together. We are better together, don't you think?"

"Of course," Angela said. "I have always wanted a community."

Jesse walked over to a man with a long, white beard who had started cooking hot dogs over a fire and was attempting to sell various food items to passers-by. He purchased two hot dogs from the salesman.

"You can't take a tour of Chicago without trying a Chicago hot dog," he said. There was no bun, but rather an old piece of bread on the verge of molding. Jesse threw the bread away before offering the hot dog to Angela.

Angela watched him become engrossed in his breakfast before tasting her own. While the food was unremarkable, simply being around him lifted her spirits. She liked how thoughtful he was and how he recognized the value in togetherness. She thought about Emi's questions about if she liked him romantically.

Jesse plucked a purple flower from the ground and put it in her curls.

Angela laughed, "But I like the yellow ones better."

"The dandelions?" he looked disgusted. "Those aren't flowers. They are weeds."

Angela frowned, "Says who? They sure look like flowers to me."

Angela picked a dandelion and examined it. It was bigger than the purple flowers, and just as bright and beautiful. She couldn't fathom why this plant would be placed in a lesser category than the other.

"The other flowers were obviously just jealous that this kind is so strong," Angela decided. She put the dandelion in her hair as well. Jesse smiled at her. They walked in silence for a while, but it was a comfortable silence.

"Jesse, I have a question," Angela finally said.

"What is it?" he responded.

"Why did you let me join The Resistance?" Angela asked. "I've kind of picked up on the fact that not just anyone is allowed to join. I think I'm the youngest person here, except for maybe Emi."

Jesse shrugged, "I guess I liked you. Besides, we are always looking for new people to join, if they are worthy."

Angela frowned. She didn't understand what made her different from the other people in the settlement — the people at the mercy of the Watch, and still in the dark about the existence of The Resistance.

"What makes a person worthy?" Angela asked.

Jesse glanced up before he spoke, "Well, you know, someone who will work hard and contribute. We do look for people with unique skills. Rain, for example, was studying medicine before she joined up. She wanted to be a pharmacist, but minored in chemistry. Her parents were mutants, I think she was hoping to cure her family, but it was too late for them. She cured her own mutation. Here at The Resistance, she has been helping Freedom create formulas to cure the man in the cage and others who live in Chicago. Zinc uses his coding skills to make our counterfeit CitCards, Emi's bubbly personality is perfect for finding recruits and communicating with patients. We use our skills to help the world. As long as you are willing to do that, you will fit in here."

Angela nodded, thinking of the fact that she had no special skills to contribute.

"This movement can only be underground for so long, you know," Jesse went on. "We have to find a way to keep our people as safe as possible once we go public. You are new, but you will be expected to help out."

"Okay. So what will my job be?" Angela asked.

"Today, Freedom will have a job assigned for you.

She will come by and let you know what that job is. So before you have to work, I just wanted you to have some fun and see the settlement."

A smile slipped onto her face. Angela couldn't think of a better way to spend the day than with Jesse.

Chapter Ten

By noon, Angela and Jesse were well on their way back home. Even without the speed of the mechanized cars, time seemed to move too fast. She didn't know if the source of this phenomenon was hanging out with Jesse or being in the settlement, but Angela wished that there were more hours in the day. The settlement was full of so many exciting places and experiences that she did not feel tired despite her lack of sleep. The excitement did not stop her mind from drifting back to her father. She wondered if her father knew about hot dogs, if he had ever seen 'the Bean,' or sat inside a Ferris wheel while it moved. He must have, at some point, if he lived here with her mother.

Jesse looked over at Angela.

"Those flowers in your hair haven't even died a

little bit. They look as vibrant as when we plucked them, maybe even better," he said.

"Maybe they like me?" Angela shrugged.

When Jesse opened the door to the warehouse, Freedom was waiting at the entrance with a grin on her face that, for once, felt genuine.

"Are you ready to hear your fate?" Freedom asked Angela.

"Ready as I'll ever be," Angela said.

"Well, come on." Freedom summoned the elevator and they all boarded the small box. When the elevator stopped, Angela noticed how quiet the halls were. She could usually hear Rain's music or Emi's loud chatter from anywhere in the basement, but not tonight. They walked into the computer room and Angela gasped in shock.

"Surprise!" various voices cheered in unison.

Zinc, Rain, and Emi were joined by Becca, Lucas, and Maria from The City Below. There were a couple of people who Angela had yet to meet, a little girl who looked about nine snuggled closely to a teenage boy who was probably her big brother. The girl's eyes glowed bright green, and Angela figured she must have some type of mutation that Rain was working to cure. She reminded Angela of the girl who was killed at the market.

"I think most of you have met our newest

member, Angela," Freedom said. "We are excited to have her here."

"Thank you," Angela said, glancing at Jesse. His grin revealed that he knew about this but didn't tell her, which made her a little annoyed. Was this why he had kept her out all night?

"Angela, your job is to help us grow our own food so we will be less dependent on buying food with our fake cards," Freedom said. "You have seen our small greenhouse in The City Below. If you need supplies, I'm sure Jesse has taught you what buildings and shops are safe to visit. And remember, stay away from the Watch. You'll start your job tomorrow. But today, get to know The Resistance. Eat. Drink. Be merry. Leave me alone."

Angela was relieved that her job did not involve any of the guns or knives she saw. She was good at gardening; she would prove herself to Freedom in no time.

There was food on the table, and drinks of both the alcoholic and nonalcoholic variety. She doubted any of her new friends would be critical of her having a drink at her own party, and poured herself a glass of wine. She took a whiff of its pungent scent before chugging it down. The drink stung her throat as she swallowed but, not wanting to appear rude, she continued to sip throughout the night.

All of the computer screens were off except for the ones used for surveillance, and Rain's radio had been moved into the control room. Instead of the hip-hop and rock Jesse's friends were usually listening to, it was playing classical music. Some of the songs were from a real piano, not the band, and Angela thought it was sweet that they had selected this music for her. It was time to celebrate with her new family away from home, but by the end of the night, her lack of sleep mixed with too many drinks caused her to walk away feeling somewhat discombobulated. She fell asleep with an overwhelming feeling of being out of place.

Angela had a strange dream that night. She was in the sky, sitting on a giant cloud. Colorful fruits and veggies floated all around her. She munched away at them. Her father was there, too, and he was eating as well. Then Angela disappeared from her own dream and her father was alone, searching for her and calling out her name. All of the fruit started to disappear around him and the cloud started to dissolve under his feet She knew her father would soon have nowhere to stand and he would fall hundreds of feet towards the ground.

"Angela!" Emi's voice cut through her dream. Angela opened her eyes and saw Emi standing over her, her eyes wide and her blue hair glowing in the dim light from the hallway.

"Wake up, I'm gonna go with you to get supplies for your job today to make sure you know what you are doing."

Angela stretched and slowly slung her feet over the edge of the bed.

"I'll meet you in the computer room," Emi said as she bounced away.

As they left The Resistance together, Emi told Angela she was taking her to a shop located in someone's home. Emi tried chatting with Angela as they walked towards this shop, but Angela was quieter than usual and offered only one-word replies to Emi's babbling.

"You look like you're in deep thought," Emi finally said. "What's up?"

"I really want to go check on my dad," Angela said. "I had a dream about him last night."

Emi chose her words carefully. "I'm sure he's fine, the Wardens rarely go out into the forests unless they are looking for someone. If you have been there for years, I doubt they are looking for him."

"I just have to see him to make sure," Angela said.

"Jesse says I have to convince Freedom I'm worth the risk, but I have a bad feeling in my gut and I want to go as soon as possible."

Emi grimaced, replying, "Well, you'd have to get permission from Freedom. You are really new to be asking for favors like that."

"I don't think she likes me very much," Angela added.

Emi shook her head in disagreement.

"She acts like that to everyone who is new. Don't worry about it," Emi said. "I know for a fact that she is excited to have you here. She didn't think Jesse would be able to find you out there."

Angela froze in her tracks.

"Find me?" Angela asked Emi. "He found me on accident. He didn't tell Freedom about me until after we made it back."

"Oh right, my mistake," Emi's face was beet red. She was quiet, which was unlike her. They walked in silence for a few moments.

"Was Jesse . . . looking for me?" Angela asked, though she knew that was impossible. No one knew she or her father existed. Her father had made sure of it by never allowing her to leave. Jesse sure made it seem as if he found her by accident. It was her choice to come with him.

"No, I just meant you were a lucky surprise," said Emi.

Angela looked down at the sidewalk as she walked. Was Emi lying? Could it be possible that Jesse was in the forest, not simply to hide from the Watch, but specifically looking for her to bring her back to Chicago with him?

It was too much to contemplate for now, but she made a mental note to get to the bottom of this later. Right now, she needed to focus on her first mission.

She looked up at the small home that they were approaching. The gray paint on the outside of the house was chipping away and the front door was broken, but there were two tiny flower pots outside and a hand painted 'welcome' sign on the door. It was clear that whoever lived here was doing all they could to make it look inviting.

"What if Freedom says I can't go see my father?" Angela asked as they approached the makeshift store.

"Then that's what's best, for now. You can't exactly run off; if you take your card with you, she can track your whereabouts on our computer. It will not show your location to the Watch, but she'll know just where you are. If you leave it behind, there is no way you'd make it back to the settlement," Emi warned.

"But why would you make the fake CitCard traceable if that's the thing you guys are fighting against?" Angela asked, frustration in her voice.

"It's to keep us safe," Emi said. "You know where we are located, so we need to know where you are. If a Warden got that information out of you, we would all be at risk of death."

"I can wait for now, but if Freedom doesn't eventually let me go, I will go back and try to find him alone. Will you help me find my father when the time comes?" Angela asked.

"You can get me into a lot of trouble with The Resistance," Emi replied, but there was compassion on her face. "But I understand that you are worried about him. Let's at least wait a week before you ask Freedom, and if she says no, I'll come with you."

Angela gave her a big hug, lifting Emi off of the ground. Emi smiled, surprised by Angela's affection.

"Also on a lighter note, you told me to tell you and now I'm telling you," Angela said. She let Emi out of her grip.

"Telling me what?" Emi asked, happy to be back on the ground.

"So, maybe I do like Jesse a little bit," Angela forced herself to say out loud.

"Oh my God!" Emi was her usually bubbly self again. "I knew it!"

They walked inside the store. The glass on the

door was shattered, but it still let out an off-tune bell sound as it was opened, alerting the homeowners so that they could come to greet their customers.

"I think he likes you, too," Emi said. "I haven't seen him this happy in a while."

The inside of the home looked more inviting than its decaying exterior. It was more home than shop, and the owner, a gray-haired woman who appeared older than her father, greeted them with a kind smile. Children's toys were scattered about the floor, which made Angela wonder if the owner, in her advanced age, had kids living in the house. Everything that was for sale was organized neatly on a table. There were only three customers in the small store, all of them older than Angela and Emi.

"There's no way they are going to notice your card is fake here," Emi reassured.

Angela got canned food items, water and chips. She also got seeds to grow vegetables and fruit in the garden. She was surprised at the high prices of water. For all of her life, water had been free.

"Why do people pay so much for *water*?" Angela asked Emi.

"It's contaminated everywhere near here. Has been for a while. No one wants to end up dead or with a mutation. All of this is imported from places far away with less pollution."

"Are you sure?" Angela had been drinking water less than thirty miles away for all of her life, and she was fine. Emi nodded as if certain, so Angela didn't argue.

Could it be possible that the lush garden where Angela had grown up was the only healthy place left near Chicago? If so, she wanted to know what made it so special and how her father happened to find it.

The doorbell rang again and a tall woman walked into the store. She had curly brown hair pulled back into a bun and wore a blue suit. A metal badge was clipped to her top.

Emi grabbed Angela's arm, pulling her over to the fruit, and focused on the tomatoes.

"What?" Angela whispered, sensing Emi's panic.

"That lady over there is a Warden," Emi said. "She's not wearing the traditional striped shirt, but I've seen her in uniform before. If she checks her radio scanner she will see less cards than people in this store."

The woman was immersed in a conversation with the owner of the home and shop.

"What should we do?" Angela asked.

"Act casual. Can you do that?" Emi asked.

"I think so," Angela whispered, but her heartbeat was starting to speed up.

Emi took Angela's shopping basket out of Angela's hands and headed over to the counter.

"Don't worry about it today. I'm good at acting natural. I'll pay for it," Emi said.

Angela nodded as they walked over to the counter. Emi waited behind the Warden, and proceeded to ask Angela casual questions about her day with Jesse.

The Warden looked back at them. "Sorry, girls, I was just checking in on an old friend. I'll be out of your way in no time." She shot Emi an apologetic smile.

"Thanks." Emi blushed and smiled up at her.

"I love your hair, by the way," the woman said to Emi. "If only I could pull that off at my age."

The Warden turned her attention away from Emi and Angela. The shop owner used a pencil and paper to add up the total of the woman's groceries and a small black scanner to scan her card and take payment. As the shop owner took the Warden's payment, the Warden looked Angela and Emi up and down with curiosity. Angela wondered if she didn't look normal enough. Were her new khakis and t-shirt too simple for her to blend in?

"I don't think I've seen you two around before," The Warden said.

"We keep to ourselves," Emi said.

The Warden nodded slowly, looking Angela over once more. She was digging in her small black purse when the shop owner handed her CitCard back.

Angela's eyes were locked on her hand, hoping she wasn't going to check her radio scanner. If Emi was thinking the same thing, she didn't show it. Angela forced her eyes to look at the bread on the counter. She could feel her face heating up.

The Warden pulled a small black object out of her purse and stepped away from the counter as Emi stepped forward. Emi watched the Warden out of the corners of her eyes while placing her groceries on the counter. Emi confidently took her fake card out of the green bag that was draped over her shoulders and handed it to the cashier. Angela avoided eye contact with the Warden or her small black item as her hands started to sweat. If they were caught, she might be killed and would never get to say goodbye to her father.

The cashier scanned the card, then handed it back to Emi.

"Thank you!" Emi flashed another bright smile.

"No problem, hon." The lady smiled back, and Emi and Angela exited the store while the Warden continued her conversation with the cashier.

"What was that in her hand?" Angela asked once safely away from the store.

"BlackBerry," Emi said.

"Fruit?" Angela was confused.

"Phone. A very ancient one, at that," Emi clarified. "I would have expected a more fashionable choice for a Warden."

They walked in thoughtful silence for a while; appreciating the fact that they still had their lives. Emi was the first to speak.

"So all your life it's just been you and your dad?" Emi asked.

"Yes," Angela said.

"Well, you're in a whole new world now. I'm like your human encyclopedia. I'll tell you anything you want to know," Emi said.

"What about school?" Angela asked, "Jesse told me it's where they taught him to read. I've been wondering if I could go."

Emi's touched her finger to her chin.

"I'm not sure how that would work with a fake CitCard. You probably won't be able to get official transcripts, but I don't think they would turn you down if you showed up wanting to learn to read," Emi said thoughtfully. "You would need to ask Freedom."

"Why don't you go to school?" Angela asked.

"School changed a lot after the war. It's not required anymore, plus I'm not carded anymore so I figured there's no point. I got rid of my official

CitCard when I joined The Resistance and devoted my life to something bigger."

Something bigger, Angela thought. But what did that truly mean to Emi? Angela was starting to feel agitated. She was tired of being given riddles about the world when she wanted concrete, absolute solutions.

"What does 'something bigger' mean to you?" Angela asked.

"To live independently of the Watch," said Emi. "People allow Kane and his Wardens to rule out of fear. If they know we have food, resources, and the ability to survive without their rule, we think humanity will choose our world over theirs. But we are not strong enough to stand up against them yet."

"I wanted to help change the world for the better, not to create a place for people who don't like it to retreat," Angela said. "If I wanted to retreat, I would have stayed home."

"We're not retreating," Emi said, her tone harsher than usual. "Sometimes, you have to create change on a small scale before you can create it on a larger one. We can heal one mutation at a time, offer food to one hungry person. You have to be patient. You don't know the things that we have had to go through to make it to where we are now, but if you want to go to school, maybe you will learn."

Chapter Eleven

"Absolutely not!" Freedom said when Angela approached her about school. "Are you trying to get yourself killed or all of us exposed?"

They were in the control room at The Resistance. Rain, Zinc, and Emi all eavesdropped intently while pretending to be distracted by various tasks.

"I know I can't get official transcripts, but —"

"The teacher at the school is paid directly by Kane and trained to report any students they are suspicious of. If they suspect your CitCard is fake you will be killed," Freedom said.

"Did you know that I can't read?" Angela asked. "I've never been taught to tell time, or given a map of the world around me. I've never been taught about the Bio Wars or any of the wars before those. If I'm really going to help the world, I need to be able to function in it."

Freedom sighed. "There may be another option."

Angela raised an eyebrow. "I'm listening."

"I know a woman," Freedom said. "Retired teacher. Tutors uncarded teens."

"Yes!" Angela exclaimed. "That would be perfect!"

"You must be willing to keep up with your responsibility as a farmer here," Freedom said sternly.

"Of course," Angela said confidently.

"Then I see no reason why not," Freedom said. "Get started on the garden tonight. Jesse, I want you to help her track the farming progress. She's still needs to learn to read and write, so I want you to go with her and write down the date and time she plants these seeds. We need to keep track of how long it takes them to grow and how much food we produce."

"Sounds good to me, my lady," Jesse said.

"And don't call me that," said Freedom as she turned and walked back towards the elevator.

Rain stood up from her chair, stretched, and wished everyone goodnight as she walked out of the room. Zinc retreated as well.

"Ready for your first night of work?" Jesse asked.

Angela took a deep breath.

"As ready as I'll ever be," she said, and they entered the tunnel that lead to the storage room.

Something was amiss. There was a loud, desperate banging coming from deep within the tunnel. The sound echoed around them. Alarmed, they raced through the darkness to the storage room door. Jesse quickly opened its metal door.

A wild and delirious Becca fell into his arms, weeping. Her arms were covered in blood and bruises. Angela could not tell if the blood was her own or someone else's. When Jesse cried out in pain from the touch of the blood on his skin, she knew the blood must be Julian's. Becca's small children and her caged husband were the only others who lived in her room. She shrieked and cried out in a language Angela didn't understand, and Jesse spoke back to her in the same language. Angela could not follow the conversation, so she looked past Jesse into the room for clues.

"Jesse, look!" Angela screamed, but Jesse was already rushing into the room where Becca's husband, Julian, lay unmoving and bleeding out on the floor, a large knife protruding from his back. Angela had never seen so much blood up close.

The two children were sitting against the wall. The older boy, Lucas, wrapped his arms around his young sister, Maria, as she cried.

"What happened?" Angela demanded.

"He was screaming out in pain, so she let him out," Jesse said. "Once free from the cage, he attacked Maria. Becca stabbed him to protect her daughter."

Angela was in shock.

"Why did he attack his own child?" she asked.

"Sometimes mutants go mad," said Jesse. "We did change his meds a bit recently, because the old dosage was not curing him. Being locked away can't help, however. Can you go get Rain?"

Angela raced back upstairs to find Rain, asleep in her bed. Angela shook her awake and explained the situation. Rain grabbed a first aid kit and rushed down to the storage room, with Angela trailing close behind. The father was clearly dead, so she treated Becca's wounds from her husband's acidic blood first and then checked on Maria. Jesse and Rain started chatting about how they would clean up his blood and get rid of the body, as if they had cleaned out dead mutants 1000 times over and it was the most normal thing in the world. Angela couldn't take much more of this; the smell of the blood and the tears of the children made her sick, and the casual talk of disposing of a person's body made her sicker. She asked Jesse if she could go upstairs.

"Okay, I think Freedom will understand if you

start your work tomorrow. I'll be up there soon; I want to make sure you are alright after seeing this," he said, his protective demeanor somehow reminding her of her father in that moment. Remembering him made her worry increase, but it wasn't the right time to bring him up again. She headed back without another word.

ANGELA WAS HAPPY TO HAVE SOME ALONE TIME with her mind. She couldn't understand how death could be so casual to Jesse or Rain. She thought about the fact that Rain's entire family was dead, and wondered if, over time, a person became numb to it. She did not want to get accustomed to death. She laughed at herself for rushing to leave home without thinking of the danger. Maybe he was right. Maybe the garden could have been her happy ending all along.

After she changed into her pajamas, which were hand-me-downs from Rain, and climbed into bed, there was a knock on her door.

"Come in," she said, pulling back her curly hair into a braid so that it wouldn't get in her face while she slept. Jesse opened the door and cautiously walked in.

"Hey," she said. "How is Becca?"

"I won't say she's fine, but she is stable. Becca and the kids are all sleeping on a cot in Rain's room tonight. We are going to get the family a proper room tomorrow. No need for them to live down there anymore, it will just remind them of who they lost," Jesse said.

"So, what's next for them?" Angela asked. "You were not able to cure him. Will the family get fake cards, become Resistance members? Will they get real cards and go out into society?"

Jesse shook his head.

"Maybe at a later point, they will get carded. For the most part, you get carded during your birth year or not at all. You can get your card removed for committing a crime, but it is hard to get carded as an adult. They would have to pass a lot of tests, " Jesse said. "As for what's next for them, I suppose that's partially up to them. They are welcome to stay with us, for now."

Angela wondered if it would be safe to tell him about her desire to run away to go visit her father. After today, could he blame her?

"Do you have any idea what you're getting yourself into?" Jesse asked.

For the briefest of moments, Angela thought Jesse was talking about her plans to run away. A panicked looked flashed onto her face. How did he know?

"Going to tutoring, I mean." Jesse added.

Angela exhaled deeply.

"They stopped enforcing school when I was young," Jesse continued. "After middle school graduation I got myself a fake CitCard to hide my identity, set my real one on fire, and joined The Resistance full time. School is just a microscopic version of everything that's wrong with society. I wish I could have gone to tutoring, instead."

"I think you just like the idea of being a rebel," Angela teased.

"You've had a traumatic night. Why don't you just stay here and spend tomorrow with me? I could teach you anything you want to know," Jesse said. He reached out his hand and placed it on top of hers. Angela felt her heart quicken, and she moved her hand away.

"Why do you do that?" Jesse asked.

"Do what?" Angela questioned, cupping her hand.

"Move away when I touch you," he asked. "Wouldn't you like to hold my hand?"

Angela un-cupped her hand, laying it back where it was on the bed. Jesse reached towards her and held her hand, stroking her palm with his thumb. Angela closed her fist over his, giving his hand a soft squeeze, and looked up and Jesse questioningly.

"Thank you for all you have done for me here," Angela said. "You didn't have to stay out all night showing me around."

"Sleep is for the weak," Jesse said.

Angela smiled at him.

"Angela, can I tell you a secret," Jesse's voice was a whisper. "If you promise not to tell anyone?"

"Of course," Angela said.

"I don't know if any of this is going to work," he said.

"Any of what?" Angela asked.

"This!" he said, his hands motioning to the surrounding room. Angela stared back blankly for a moment before she understood.

"Any of the work you do with The Resistance? Why would you join if you felt that way?"

"We have good intentions, but more mutants die in our basement than we are able to cure. Meanwhile, President Kane keeps hiring more Wardens to keep everyone in line and kill everyone he deems undesirable. We are trying to save the world with big guns and small gardens, but we don't know what the hell we are doing."

Angela looked into his eyes, trying to figure him

out. How could he live life working for a cause he believed was hopeless?

"Less than one percent of the earth's total population survived the Bio Wars. Humans are basically an endangered species. Sure, we are rebuilding, but according to Freedom, we are at two percent of what we once were. The Bio Wars were decades ago and people are still getting sick or mutating. I think the world died a long, long time ago," Jesse went on. "We are just living in its dust. It's like a dead body decaying into the ground. Once something starts to die, it rarely will come back. We can't fight fate."

Jesse's face was tense. Angela tried to think of the right words to offer, but knew she would likely come up short.

"How do you know?" Angela finally asked. "Two percent is better than one. The fact that I am here in this settlement, away from everything I have ever known, is the result of me deciding to fight fate. I didn't know if anyone else was alive, but I trusted you."

"Not your smartest moment, was it?" he teased and smiled at her. "But I guess something good has come out of me joining up. I got to meet you."

"Just remember," Angela continued. "If you put limits on the world, or limits on yourself, that's the *only* way to insure nothing good will ever happen. I still believe there are happy endings left in this world. Don't give up on yourself before the world has given up on you. There is time to find your happy ever after."

Angela squeezed his hand tighter. She decided not to tell him about her plans to visit home. He would probably value her safety more than the promise of bringing her father to Chicago, seeing as he didn't think anything they were doing would work. Was she the only true believer in a better world? Still, she didn't want him to go. She liked being around him, and he seemed to like being around her.

"I have one more secret," Jesse said. His voice sounded unsure, hesitant. For once, he looked more nervous than she felt. Angela smiled at him, hoping to reassure him.

"Sure." Angela was glad that he could stay a little longer.

"I've been wanting to try this," he said.

Angela watched, wide eyed, as Jesse moved closer. He reached his hand to her temple and brushed a few stray strands of hair behind her ear. Wherever his fingers touched, he left a trail of electricity. He pulled her closer to him, then paused for a brief moment, his lips only inches away from hers, and studied her eyes to see how she felt about him closing that gap. She offered a small nod and he moved in, his lips delicately grazing across her own. In only a few heartbeats his kiss grew in intensity and his movements became confident and determined.

The butterflies in Angela's stomach were in full force. She could feel his breathing and smell his warm scent. He wrapped his arms around her waist and pull her closer. She reached out and held him tight.

There was a knock at the door. They flinched away from each other.

"Come in," Angela called, staring open-mouthed at the door. Emi walked in with a backpack in her hand.

Emi's eyes went from Angela to Jesse, who were both blushing.

"Oh," Emi said. "Did I interrupt something here?"

"No," Angela said. "We were just talking."

"Uh huh," Emi said, but she did not look convinced. "Well, this is my old backpack from school. I put some paper and pens inside . . . also, a few books to help you learn to read and write letters. They are meant for young kids, but should work. It should help with tomorrow."

"Thank you," Angela said politely.

"Well, I'm going to go." She glanced from Angela to Jesse, offering Angela a small wink before she scurried away.

Angela couldn't help but chuckle as Emi rushed

out of the room. She slowly looked back up at Jesse. With just one kiss, the nature of their relationship shifted. She wasn't sure how to navigate this new bond.

"I think I should go, too. You need your rest. Big day tomorrow," Jesse said.

"Yeah," Angela agreed quickly. "Good night."

Jesse rushed towards the door but paused before leaving. He looked back at her and smiled.

"Thank you," he said.

"For what?" Angela asked.

"For being my happy ever after."

Chapter Twelve

Angela woke at the crack of dawn, her body too on edge to rest any longer. Whenever she would try to go back to sleep, her mind would wander to Jesse's kiss or Julian's dead body. It was all too much for one night.

She crawled out of her warm blanket, searched her closet for clean clothes, and tried to pretend it was just another day. Deep down, she felt today was immensely important. By meeting this tutor, she was taking her first steps towards becoming a functioning adult.

She pulled her baby blue dress over her tired body, picked up Emi's backpack, and slipped on scandals. Right before she stepped out of the room she heard a knock at the door. Jesse peaked inside.

"Need me to walk you to your tutor, Angela?" he asked.

"I thought you didn't like school," she teased as she marched past him out the door. She wanted to spend time with him, but part of her felt she needed to do this alone.

"It's not school. Besides, I thought you might like the company," he said.

"I'm fine. Really. I'll see you tonight," Angela said, wanting to be alone with her thoughts. Freedom told her where the tutor lived, and she didn't want Jesse to think she was not capable of taking care of herself.

"Okay," he said, looking disappointed.

Angela moved closer to him and planted a small kiss on his lips. A crooked grin spread across his face. He reached out and pulled her into a deeper embrace, but she moved away before he could persuade her.

"Bye everyone!" Angela called out to anyone who happened to be listening as she summoned the old elevator. She didn't wait for a response before she hopped on.

IT WAS A SUNNY DAY, BUT THE WIND WAS BLOWING with all its strength. Angela enjoyed walking because it gave her time alone to think and observe the world around her.

To get to the tutor's home, Angela had to walk past the settlement's schoolhouse. A few windows of the schoolhouse were shattered, but beyond that, the grounds looked like they were still being cared for. Dozens of carded teens waited outside the large brick building, chatting amongst themselves as they waited for their teacher to arrive and unlock the door.

Two blocks past the schoolhouse, Angela turned down a narrow, littered alleyway to a small house painted a dull yellow. Angela wasn't sure if she was in the correct place. At one point in history, there were more than a million homes in Chicago. Even with the majority of those households having been destroyed, there were still enough structurally sound buildings in the settlement to allow everyone to claim a decent home. Some people moved into apartments or hotel rooms, while others found houses to call home. But almost everyone picked locations with neighbors nearby.

This house was at the end of a cul-de-sac of abandoned homes that were all too modest and unremarkable to inspire anyone to claim them. Angela was surprised the tutor would call this area home. After making sure the numbers on the door matched the numbers Freedom had shown her, Angela pulled open the dented screen and knocked on a wood door covered in cracked yellow paint.

A woman with copper-colored skin and long, silver locs opened the door. She wore a bright, flowing multicolored skirt and a fitted green top.

"Come in child," the woman said. "Freedom told me to expect you. You must be Angela. I'm Miss Kaper."

Angela smiled. "Thank you for inviting me into your home."

"It's always nice to see young people who are excited about learning," the woman said.

Angela stepped into the room and was overwhelmed by a thick fragrance emitting from the dozens of incense burning in the room. That's one way to block out the pungent stench of the air outside, she thought. These was no generator to power the room, so Miss Kaper had lanterns in the places that sunlight didn't reach. The room was sparsely furnished, but the walls were covered in photographs of high school graduates, flyers advertising talent shows, musicals, sporting events, and proms. Angela knew these photographs were mementos from the past like the items in her father's box back home.

"Happy to be here," Angela responded.

A teenage girl sat on the couch wrapped in a blanket. Her eyes lit up at the sight of Angela.

"I knew about you before she did," the girl said in a singsong voice.

She had long wavy hair in a reddish-golden shade that contrasted against her tan skin. Her eyes were green and striking, and in the white of her left eye there was what looked like a small tattoo of a star.

"You just moved to the settlement a few days ago, right?" the girl asked.

"I'm sorry . . . who are you?" Angela asked. How did she know when she got to Chicago?

"I'm Violet," she said. "I know your friend, Jesse."

"Did he tell you about me?" Angela asked.

"No," Violet said. "I haven't spoken to Jesse in years."

Angela narrowed her eyes at the girl, but was unsure how to respond.

"Enough, girls," Miss Kaper said. "You are both here to learn."

Miss Kaper shared that she was a teacher years ago, but was fired for refusing to report uncarded students to the Watch. Angela asked her what the school in the settlement was like.

Even though school was no longer required, Miss Kaper said dozens of students still attended. The students were motivated by the dream of getting into one of the few colleges that still existed, a sure-fire ticket out of their birth settlement and to a better, or at least more interesting, world. the Watch was hesitant to let people leave Chicago for reasons other than work or education. By keeping everyone in their birth settlements, the Watch could easily keep track of the population and the amount of aid needed at each location.

After leaving the school, she started tutoring students who, for one reason or another, could not attend school. She purposely chose this neighborhood because of its seclusion.

"I couldn't risk going to a real school," Violet said. "If anyone finds out about my mutations, they would call the Watch on me."

Angela's eyes widened, "You're a mutant?" She had never had the chance to speak with a mutant before.

"Want to see my ability?" Violet asked. Miss Kaper looked annoyed, but Angela nodded.

Violet reached out her hand towards Angela and when Angela took it, a jolt of electricity shot through her body."

"Ow!" Angela yelped. "What the heck?"

"Cool, right?" Violet said. "And that's just one of my abilities."

"Enough Violet," Miss Kaper said. "Angela is here to learn."

Angela explained that she wanted to learn to read and write. Miss Kaper spent the majority of the day tutoring Angela, teaching her what sounds each letter made and a few basic sight words, including street names and places around the settlement. At the end of the day, after stepped outside of Miss Kaper's home, Angela pulled Violet aside.

"How did you know when I came to the Chicago?" Angela challenged.

"Some people can see a little more clearly than others and understand a little bit more than most," Violet said. "You could say I have a really special mind."

"Is that your other mutation?" Angela asked.

"Quiet!" Violet whispered. "I don't really like to call it that, I just have a brain that works a little bit differently. My cousin Winter has a similar brain, but her powers are much stronger than mine. She was the one who told me about you."

"How did you meet Jesse?" Angela asked.

"In middle school, all of our friends use to hang out at this arcade and bowling place called Glee. We didn't know it, but there were people doing recruiting there."

"Recruiting for what?" Angela asked.

"I think you know what," Violet said. "That was when he met Freedom."

"You know about The Resistance!" Angela blurted out. So much for it being a top-secret underground movement.

Violet ignored Angela and continued, "I think Jesse had a little crush on Freedom at first. He was thirteen and she was seventeen at the time. No way she was interested."

Violet rolled her eyes.

"So he joined and you didn't?" Angela asked, pulling the entire story together in her head.

Violet nodded. "Tomorrow after tutoring, I would like you to meet Winter. She can explain more."

And with that, Violet rushed off. Angela decided to call it a day and make her way home.

Chapter Thirteen

The distance between Miss Kaper's house and The Resistance was great, but Angela did not mind. It offered an opportunity to dream.

As she traversed the desolate streets, she imagined the settlement in its prime, when it was a bustling city. She pictured hundreds of cars racing past the tall, strong buildings. She saw a boarded-up strip mall and imagined prom dress shopping with Emi before taking Jesse to the dance. As she passed a blocked entrance to the L, she imagined hopping on a crowded bus or train and traveling to the lake with Zinc and Rain. When she made it back home, her dad would be sitting on the porch with a brand new Wild West book in hand, waiting to lecture her about coming home on time after a night of hanging out with friends.

Back at the abandoned warehouse, Angela wanted to collapse onto her bed and rest her tired muscles. She desired time to herself to think about her conversation with Violet and to center her mind. She could not shake the feeling that The Resistance knew more about her than they were letting on, that her encounter with Jesse was not by chance alone. But she still had a job to do if she was to keep her home and prove herself to Freedom. She was in charge of the garden, and it was her first day.

Angela looked for Jesse because she remembered that he was supposed to track her progress, but he was nowhere to be found. When she decided to check her own bedroom, she saw Becca and Freedom standing inside.

"Hey." Angela was confused. Why was her room being invaded?

"Hey!" Freedom seemed startled. "Angela, there have been some changes."

Angela put her hands on her hips, summoning the courage to look Freedom in the eyes.

"Okay. What type of changes?" Angela asked.

"Becca and her little ones need a place to stay, so you are going to be switching places with them for a while," Freedom said.

"Switching places?" Angela wasn't sure what she meant.

"It's just temporary, until we find Becca and her children a permanent home," Freedom said. "You will live in the storage room downstairs. We will let you out each morning to attend tutoring and do any errands you need. We think it will be a positive change overall; the greenhouse is down there and it will allow you to be closer to your work."

Angela frowned. There were plenty of unoccupied or minimally occupied rooms upstairs. Why couldn't they move some storage boxes out of the way and let her sleep in one of them? And what did they mean by "let her out?" Would they not allow her to have a key? She was fully capable of letting herself out. Why were they treating her like a prisoner?

"Where is Jesse?" Angela felt more comfortable expressing her discomfort to him. He would not allow this.

"He will be down to track your work. You may go get started," Freedom said, handing her a key. Angela knew arguing with her was useless. She took the key and entered the tunnel that lead to the basement alone for the first time, but she vowed to not let anyone leave her inside the storage room without a key.

Since Becca and her children were living upstairs

and Jesse wasn't here yet, she decided to explore her new home office a bit. She tried to turn on one of the computers, but soon realized she was clueless when it came to operating technology. Instead, she started to dig around the file cabinets in the room and look at the papers inside. Paper was something that she understood. The file cabinet that held the papers reminded her of her father's boxes. She recognized some of the letters on the file from tutoring, but was still unable to read any of the words beyond a few sight words that she remembered. A few of them had photographs attached to the documents with staples or paper clips.

On one file, she saw a picture of the girl with glowing eyes from the party, on another was a picture of Julian. There were hundreds and hundreds of files, and more pictures than there were people in the city. Angela realized that these documents spanned many years and some of the people must be long dead. She found herself imagining the lives of the people in the picture and wishing she could understand the words, when she saw an image that made her heart stop.

One top one of the files, attached by a tiny metal paperclip, there was a photo of a woman. Brown skin. Dark hair in coils. A familiar smile.

Angela's mother.

She gasped, dropping the stack of papers from

her hand, and began to panic. Why did The Resistance have a picture of her *mother* stored away? It was becoming increasingly unlikely that Jesse had found her on accident.

ANGELA COULD NOT READ THE WORDS ON THE FILE, so she picked up and folded the paper and stuffed it inside her dress pocket. She quickly tried to clean up the mess she had made in the room. After she was certain that everything looked the same as it did before, she walked over to the garden and started planting the seeds. A heartbeat later, the door swung open and Jesse waltzed into the room.

"Hey, I see you are already hard at work. How was tutoring?" he asked, reaching out towards her to give her a hug.

Angela shifted to avoid his arms, but acted as if she had not noticed his attempt to embrace her. Angela tried to act casual. He looked so genuinely happy to see her that she didn't want to believe he had any ulterior motives for bringing her to Chicago, but photos don't lie.

"Tutoring was fine." Angela didn't want him to know she had met Violet. She wanted to decide if she should talk to Winter herself.

"Were there any other students?" He asked.

"Yep." Angela was purposely vague.

"Make any new friends?" Jesse asked. He sounded like a prying parent, and she wondered if living with Jesse would be much different than staying home.

"Yes." Angela said curtly. Then, when she saw concern in Jesse's eyes, she decided to offer a little more. "A mutant. She zapped me."

Jesse looked at Angela with mischief in his eyes.

"I missed you while you were away," he said, pulling her closer until their faces were only inches apart. Even though she suspected he was lying to her, that he knew more than he was letting on, when he pulled her near her heart raced, betraying the logical part of her mind. Her mind went back to the first kiss, her lips eager to taste his again, but with the information she knew now, she wondered how could she possibly want to kiss him.

"You're not going to run off on me with any of the boys from your tutoring class, are you?" Jesse's voice was a deep whisper.

Angela giggled. There were no boys in her tutoring class.

"They're not my type," Angela whispered back, cursing herself when the words left her lips. Was she flirting with him?

Jesse smiled at her and wrapped his arms around

her waist. Slowly, he moved his lips to hers. When Jesse kissed her, all thoughts of the file seemed to fade away. Her mind and heart were consumed by desire. Down here, there was no one to interrupt their embrace. Angela held him closer as they kissed, and when he finally pulled his lips away, she felt like they were worlds apart.

When he removed his arm from her waist, the distance allowed her to regain a bit of her sanity. Her mother's file flashed back into her mind. She needed to get the truth out of him.

"Would you ever lie to me?" Angela blurted out.

"Of course not," Jesse said, taken aback. "I love you."

And with those words, he started to move in for another kiss. But Angela was frozen. She could not love him, at least not until she knew the truth.

"I need time to think," Angela said.

"I . . . uh . . . I understand," he said, trying to force words out of his mouth, but not knowing what to say. His voice was confused and stricken, his face looked pained. "I'm sorry if I moved too fast —"

"Let's just work on the garden," Angela said, and they directed their attention to planting seeds. The room was silent, but it wasn't the comfortable silence they usually shared.

After she was done with her work and Jesse had recorded all of the items she had planted and harvested on a file, Angela asked him if it would be okay if she could sleep upstairs.

"Sorry," Jesse said. "Freedom says you have to sleep down here tonight. I will be taking your key, but I will let you out for tutoring in the morning."

She glanced over at the cage, still waiting for a new occupant. Being locked right outside of the cage was not much different than being locked inside it. She would have to think fast.

"I don't really feel safe alone down here." Angela moved closer to Jesse, reaching out to hold his hand. "I keep thinking of Julian's body. It's stuck in my mind."

Jesse nodded. "I can sleep here with you tonight, if you need me to."

Angela realized that was as good of an offer as she would get. He could not leave her trapped down here forever if he was here too, and she would not have to part with her key.

The storage room was cold, and Jesse suggested that they cuddle up close to stay warm. Angela turned him down, opting for her own blanket. She shivered throughout the night.

Angela's dreams were haunted by images of her

father, only his hair was dull and gray. There were bags under his bloodshot eyes as he searched the empty kitchen cabinets for food. Eventually, he ran from the house, through the garden, and leapt over the gate. He disappeared into the dark and dangerous wilds.

The next morning Angela woke to find Jesse examining the tiny garden. Angela was surprised to see that most of the seeds had already sprouted.

"Some green thumb you have," Jesse smiled at her, all too dismissive of something akin to a miracle. This soil was taken from within the settlement. If it was this easy to grow food, why were so many people hungry?

"Right . . . " Angela said, watching the buds in amazement and remembering the berries that grew overnight in the forest. "How long does it usually take crops to grow?"

"Depends on the crop. The corn we planted typically would take at least a couple of months, if it grew at all," Jesse explained.

Was there something special about these seeds in particular that caused them to grow while the settlement struggled to find food?

"So, are you going to let me out for tutoring?" Angela asked, trying to sound casual, even though she was sure she wasn't coming back. There was no way she would let anyone lock her away again. She needed to get to her father.

Jesse unlocked the door, and she gave him a kiss on the cheek before walking away. He frowned, obviously hoping for more.

She arrived at the Miss Kaper's home early and knocked on the door before Violet got there. Miss Kaper opened the door in tattered pajamas and informed her that she was an hour early, in case she hadn't noticed. Angela asked Miss Kaper if she would help her read something, and pulled the file with her mother's picture on it out of her pocket.

The document notes said that a woman named Florence was treating her mother, Aliyah Fields, for a mutation. Her mutation caused her to become hypersensitive to her environment, draining toxins from the plants and animals around her. If those plants and animals were sick and diseased, as most were during the wars, she would catch the sickness while the plants or animals became well. The drugs used to treat her mutation had positive results throughout her pregnancy, but after she had her child, the illness came back and Aliyah died. The document noted that the baby tested positive for a mutation as well, but it didn't specify any more information about the baby. The file said, "Further studies were to be done on the subject."

"How did you find this?" the teacher asked.

Angela realized she was "the subject," and that she would have to tread carefully if she wanted to prevent any more studies from taking place on her. She didn't want the Watch getting called to silence the supposed mutant. Then again, Miss Kaper had sacrificed a relatively easy life as a teacher to help mutants. Angela doubted she would turn her in.

"I think she's my mother," Angela said.

Miss Kaper looked at the woman in the picture.

"She sure does look like you," she observed.

Angela took the file and put it back in her pocket. She started fidgeting with her watch.

"Are you in any kind of trouble?" Miss Kaper asked, looking genuinely concerned. Angela decided not to share the entire story. She was a hundred percent certain that Jesse knew who she was when he stumbled upon her garden, and therefore doubted her ability to be a good judge of character.

"No," Angela said. "But my father might be."

All of the pieces of the puzzle were coming together, and Angela felt like she had been pulled into a tornado that had been chasing her for days. She could barely breathe. The strange occurrences that happened to her were starting to make sense: the dreams about her father, the blueberry bush bearing fruit when she slept near it, the seeds sprouting overnight. If her mother had a mutation while she was pregnant with Angela, it makes sense that Angela might have a mutation too. If her mutation was keeping her garden healthy, how long until her home was just as barren as the rest of the world?

"Is there any way I can help?" Miss Kaper asked, moving away from the doorway so Angela could enter her home.

"No," Angela said. "I'll have to talk to my father"

"Well, okay," Miss Kaper said. "Let me finish getting ready for tutoring. If you ever need anything, let me know."

As Angela waited for Violet to arrive, she started to think of her father again. She wished she had talked to him about leaving first and told him good-bye. Seeing as the Wardens were eager to kill anyone with a mutation, it was easy to see why he kept her away from other people. But why did he keep her in the dark about her mutation this entire time? She decided that she didn't regret leaving; she just wished things had turned out better. She was proud of her bravery, but what had it cost her father? Without her, was he starving?

Violet arrived, and they continued their tutoring sessions as normal. After tutoring, Violet stopped Angela before she had a chance to walk out of the door.

"Remember, we are meeting Winter today," she said.

"Right," Angela said.

"She said she'll meet us near the schoolhouse to talk," Violet said, grabbing Angela by the arm and pulling her along.

By the time Angela and Violet approached the schoolhouse, all of the students had left. There was a woman sitting under a tree, so small she might be confused for a teen. This woman had dark brown hair, brown eyes, and light brown skin. A hopeful smile filled her face when she saw Angela approach.

"Hello." The woman stood up and shook Angela's hand.

"Hello. Winter?" Angela asked.

"I'm so excited to meet you," Winter said.

"Is she the one? From your dream?" Violet whispered to Winter excitedly.

"She sure looks like it, but there is only way to be certain," Winter said, handing Angela a couple of seeds.

"Plant them tonight," Winter said, "Keep it near you when you sleep. Can you do that for me?"

Angela laughed, "I'm way ahead of you."

"Oh?" Winter said.

"You want to know if they will sprout overnight," Angela said. "And they will."

Winter leaned closer to Angela, asking, "Do you know what you are?"

"No," Angela admitted. "But I am learning. Quickly. I know that my mother could absorb toxins from the environment, as if her body was desperate to suck the sickness out of the world. It killed her. I'm not sure if it will kill me, too."

"Do you feel sick?" Winter asked.

Angela shook her head. "I feel fine."

"You are not your mother," Winter said.

"My mother could make plants healthy, just like me," Angela said.

"She absorbed toxins, like a sponge. We think you convert toxins. Your body turns it into something useful, something that doesn't hurt you. "

Angela didn't understand.

"When we breathe out, we rid ourselves of carbon dioxide because too much of it is toxic to us. Plants convert it into something they need. There are many life forms that detoxify their environments by absorbing radioactive substances, heavy metals, or toxic chemicals. But when a human has an ability like that, it's a miracle," Winter said.

"You mean a mutation?" Angela clarified.

"All of evolution is a mutation or a miracle, Angela," Winter said. "It depends on how you look at it."

"How did you know who I am?" Angela asked.

"You are not the only girl with a gift. I have been given the gift of prophecy," Winter explained. "Violet has a similar gift, but mine told me you would come into our lives."

"Are you guys carded?" Angela asked.

"Yes," Violet said.

"How are you able to get a card with a mutation?"

Winter smiled mischievously, "Not all mutations show up in tests. They never notice mine."

"My second mutations didn't develop until I was older," Violet said. "I already had a card at that point. I just avoid going to school or to the doctor. That makes me pretty much like every other teenager."

Winter giggled.

"Did The Resistance try to recruit you?" Angela asked.

"I had no desire to join. I support The Resistance," Winter explained cautiously, "but I don't agree with their methods. They believe the ends always justify the means, no matter who is kidnapped, or caged, or dead. We do not lie, cheat, or kill. If we did, what makes us any better than the Watch? Our biggest difference is that The Resistance seems to think mutants should be cured, unless they are useful, like you are. Then, they should be exploited. We don't believe mutants should be cured, or used. All should live in peace."

Angela nodded. "How did you know about me?"

"I dreamt of you for the first time three years ago," Winter said. "I didn't think much of it at the time. You looked a lot younger, about thirteen, and you were gardening. I didn't think it was real at first. Most of my visions take place in locations that I recognize as reality. Your garden was *unreal.* I thought it was just a dream at the time, but I kept having them. The problem was, my dreams never offered any clue as to where you, or that beautiful garden, were located. I asked around, hoped and prayed, looked at maps, but still had no clue how to find you. Until one day, I had a dream in which you and a boy drove into the city. This dream took place months ago, but I had a feeling it was going to happen soon."

Angela was silent, thoughtful.

"So I am a mutant?" Angela needed to hear someone else say it.

"You are," said Winter.

"That explains a lot," Angela admitted, but her dreams of a peaceful, legal life with her father would be unattainable now.

"I have yet to see what happens next, but I believe you will play a role in the liberation of this land," Winter said. "I would love for you to visit my home sometime. I run a Lighthouse."

"Like for boats?" Angela asked.

"Not exactly. It's just what we call houses like mine, a safe house of sorts for people who don't feel safe. Only, no cures, no cages," she said.

"I will think about it," Angela said. "I have to go."

Violet smiled at Angela. "Safe journeys."

Chapter Fourteen

Unwilling to be confined to the storage room, Angela decided she would not go home that night. She made her way to the beach near Navy Pier instead, and sat on the sands her mother had sat upon years before Angela's birth. Eventually, Angela walked over to the pier and climbed into the lowest seat of the Ferris wheel. Sprawled out against the cool metal, the sides of the pods kept her hidden as she closed her eyes and drifted off to sleep, dreaming of the wheel carrying her up into the sky.

The next morning, the sky looked cloudy and the air smelled of rain. Angela rushed to Miss Kaper's home, but the rain started while she was on her way and she was soaked before she got there. Miss Kaper looked concerned as Angela stumbled into the room, late and wet.

"I have spare clothes if you ever need them," Miss Kaper said as Angela plopped down on an empty beanbag. Angela spent her morning with the teacher, wrapped in a blanket and learning to read. She could sense the teacher's concern, but she didn't want to drag anyone else into her problems.

After tutoring, Violet asked why she was wearing the same clothes for the third day in a row, and why they were so damp.

"I didn't go home last night," Angela admitted. "They want to keep me locked inside a storage room, with their garden."

Violet nodded, concern in her eyes. "You should stay with Winter,"

"I honestly don't know who to trust," Angela said. "Everybody wants something from me. Why would Winter be any different?"

"We all want something from each other. It's part of being part of humanity. But, I think what she wants is to know that she was able to help you," Violet said. "She will have some clean clothes and a place for you to stay."

Angela forced a smile. She appreciated the help, but getting back to her father was still of utmost importance to her at that moment. At the same time, if Winter really did have a prophetic mind, it wouldn't hurt to pay her a visit. Maybe her visions could help Angela find her father. She decided to take Violet up on her offer.

Chapter Fifteen

Angela and Violet assumed that The Resistance was likely already looking for their lost captive, so they took a scenic route to Winter's home. As they walked through alleys and side streets to avoid more popular roads, Angela took the opportunity to learn more about Violet's family.

Violet's father lived in apartments near Navy Pier. She visited him often. Her mother and brother had passed away years ago.

"My brother . . . he mutated," Violet said. "It made him violent, and all the cures we found made it worse. My mom actually ended his life. It's not something I like to think about."

Angela thought of how Becca must have felt when she took her husband's life to protect her child. She understood why The Resistance wanted to find cures just as much as she understood why Winter didn't want to find them.

"Did it hurt when they put that star in your eye?" Angela finally asked, deciding to change the subject.

"Oh, that? It's a birthmark," Violet explained. There was lightness in her voice, as if she was accustomed to answering this question.

Angela eyes got wide, "But it's a perfect star, with five points. And it's red. Your eyes are green."

Violet just shrugged.

They approached a small, inconspicuous home. The walls were painted blue and the grass, while yellow, was trimmed. Pots that held artificial flowers sat on both sides of the front door. Violet knocked and Winter answered.

"Come in!" Winter exclaimed, then rushed back to the stove. "It's so good to see you."

The front door opened upon a kitchen and dining area. Winter was making something that smelled delicious in a pot on the stove, reminding Angela of how hungry she was. The dining area had been converted into a small, cozy living space. Instead of a kitchen table, there was a long, low table near a loveseat and a small television. A collage of pictures of family and friends behind the television.

"You have a beautiful home," Angela said,

meaning every word. It was the coziest place she had seen since coming to Chicago. The room felt lived-in. There were various items scattered about in incorrect locations — art supplies, tools, and sweet-smelling soaps — as if everything that didn't have a place to be was welcomed in this living room. Angela would soon learn that displaced people were also included.

"Thanks. I call this place my sanctuary. I didn't know if you'd actually come. I hoped you would, of course," Winter said.

"Why didn't you think I would come?" Angela asked.

"I didn't know if I scared you away," Winter said with a shrug. "Follow me, my young apprentice, I have a safe space where you can stay. Welcome to the Lighthouse."

There was a long hallway between the kitchen and dining area, through which Winter lead Angela. They arrived at a larger living area with a couch, loveseat, and a stack of sleeping bags up against the wall.

There were five people in the room, and they spanned a wide range of ages. They were unified in the warmth and kindness they treated Angela with as soon as she walked into the room. Angela appreciated meeting Winter's friends, but all she wanted to do was check on her father. She wondered if Winter's ability to foretell the future could help.

"You mentioned being able to see . . . beyond what is there. Can you see my garden?" asked Angela.

"My visions come when they choose," Winter said. "I have not seen your home since you've come to Chicago."

Angela started fidgeting with the watch on her wrist. The pitch of her voice heightened as she asked, "Why did you have a vision of me anyway? Do you always have visions about strangers?"

"No, usually it's people I know. Sometimes I experience a bit of deja vu and see people I have yet to meet. When I saw you and that healthy garden, my first thought was that I was having a vision of some place in the past," Winter said. "My great-grandfather signed up for one of those Advanced Bioengineering studies. They gave him some type of injection that altered the cells of his brain. After that, he would experience intuitions that always seemed to turn out right. My mom got them, too. That's how Violet's mind works, as well. I think I'm the only person in my family who actually has visions."

Angela sat down on the edge of the couch.

"My father is there without me, and I need to go back and see him right away. I need to make sure he is okay, and I can't help but feel like time is running out. I don't know how long it will take for all of the food to die."

"I understand," Winter said. "Do you know the way back home?"

"No," Angela sighed. "But Jesse does. I will have to go back to The Resistance tomorrow to convince him to come with me."

Winter nodded, "I have to stay here and host the guests, but if need be, Violet can go with you back to The Resistance."

"Guests?" Angela asked.

"There are many people who call the Lighthouse home, and more who visit because they enjoy the company," Winter said. "This room will be full by tonight."

Angela looked around the room and noticed a quote mounted on the wall. The large frame dominated the room.

"What does that say?" she asked Winter, pointing up at the quote.

"I will bring my people Israel back from exile. They will rebuild the ruined cities and live in them. They will plant vineyards and drink their wine, they will make gardens and eat their fruit," Winter answered, without even looking up at the words to read them.

Angela walked closer to the framed quote, both drawn to and confused by the words.

"It's a quote from the Bible," Winter explained. "One of my favorite verses."

"Bible?" asked Angela.

"It's one of the old holy books," she said. "I like the reminder that once something is gone, it can come back stronger, be rebuilt."

"Isn't religion banned?" Angela asked.

"It is," Winter shrugged. "But I am not a fan of censorship."

Violet led Angela to a large bookshelf that held ten times the amount of books in her father's old boxes.

"We have collected a lot of holy books here, as well as the works of philosophers, artists, and thought leaders of the past," Violet explained. "There are people who still practice the old religions, no matter what the Watch says. Winter, for example, is a Christian."

"Do you practice any of them?" Angela asked.

"I don't practice a particular faith, but I think it's so important that people can choose to think or do as they please. Come, let me make you a bed. You will understand what I meant by Lighthouse when the guests arrive later."

"I try to make my house a safe place for people to come to talk about things they could not discuss otherwise. Banned books, policed thoughts," Winter said. "We want to keep the world our ancestors called home alive, in some way. A place like this allows debate and discussion of many ideas that you would not find discussed elsewhere in the settlement."

"What if people disagree?" Angela asked.

"They are allowed to do that," Winter said. "Truth doesn't force itself."

Angela walked over to the large bookshelf and started browsing the books. She settled on one with more pictures than words. After flipping through the pages, she gawked at a photo of a tiny village hidden behind a small cliff. The most striking aspect of the photo was the sky, the way the stars seemed to dance within the dark night.

"Moon babies," Angela mumbled to herself, thinking of her first night in the forest with Jesse.

"Van Gogh was a creative genius, yeah?" Winter said. "His paintings still exist, somewhere out there. the Watch don't really value art, but still, it's gotta be worth a fortune. You know they don't even teach about artists anymore in what's left of schools and universities? It's a shame."

They heard a knock at the door, and Winter ran off to answer it. One by one, strangers trickled in. Soon, the living room was full of visitors.

That night, there were more people in Winter's living room than in the entirety of the market.

Crammed wall-to-wall, some people studied various religious texts and philosophies, while others simply enjoyed each other's company. They traded food, clothing, and other resources, alongside laughter.

Angela's heart pounded in fear when she saw a familiar face among the crowd; it was the female Warden with the BlackBerry, from the store. Some of these books were illegal to own. Could she be here to arrest or kill all of Winter's guests?

Angela pulled Winter aside. Lowering her voice, she spoke, "That women over there," Angela motioned to the woman as she chatted with a group of people, "I have seen her before. She is a Warden!"

"I know. She comes all the time," Winter said. "She is not the only Warden to attend."

"Are the guests here carded?" Angela asked.

"Yes," Winter assured. "As far as I know, at least."

"She kills people!" Angela exclaimed. She had seen how nonchalantly the Watch took lives. "Carded or not, she could kill all of these people just for being here, just for reading these books."

Winter looked thoughtful, "Well, she hasn't done it yet."

Annoyed by Winter's dismissive attitude, Angela took a seat on a couch and decided to observe the people, keeping an eye on the Warden.

Soon, her attention was drawn to a man who was

humming and strumming an acoustic guitar. Angela knew what the instrument was from her father's stories, but had never seen one or heard one being played. She enjoyed the melodious vibrations of the strings as they were strummed softly. As the man filled the room with warm music, a small group of people gathered around him. Watching him play made her miss her piano. Angela moved closer, listening to the melody as the group started to hum and sing:

"I am a poor wayfaring stranger
Traveling through this world alone
Yet there's no sickness, no toil, nor danger
In that bright land to which I go

I'm going there to see my Father
I'm going there no more to roam
I'm only going over Jordan
I'm only going over home"

While Angela did not know the words, she started to hum along with the music. Though parts of the lyrics sounded sad to Angela, the happiness in which the man sang them transformed the tune into a joyful song. This was the first time music from the settlement had moved her so much, if not more, than the sounds of her piano.

Angela glanced over at the Warden, who was sitting on the ground and slowly rocking with the tune of the guitar. Tentatively, Angela approached her.

"Mind if I sit here?" Angela asked, motioning to an empty spot on the carpeted floor.

"Sure," the Warden said. "Beautiful music, don't you think."

"It sounds so peaceful," Angela agreed. "I can't remember the last time I've felt so calm."

The guitarist took a break from singing but continued to strum his instrument, allowing the crowd to hum along with the tune.

"You're a Warden, right?" Angela asked.

"Yes," the woman said. "I remember you. Your friend had such pretty hair."

"Why did you join the Watch?" Angela asked, her curiosity getting the best of her. What could drive *anyone* to want to join such a horrible group?

The woman leaned back and looked up, closing her eyes and swaying her head to the tune. At first Angela thought she was ignoring her, but then her lips parted.

"The same reason anyone does, I guess," she said. "The benefits from Kane don't hurt, but at the end of the day I just want to help keep people safe."

The Warden paused, but Angela said nothing, sensing there was more to the story. Eventually, the Warden continued, "I believe the world can be like it was before the Bio Wars again. People were healthy, happy, and fully human. We had enough food and water. We never had to worry about random mutant attacks. In the old days, people lived by the law and felt safe enough to do as they please."

Angela nodded, but couldn't help seeing flaws in the women's logic. Sure, there were people like Emi and Jesse who chose not to live by the law, but they only made that choice because of people who never had the option to. If you were a mutant, your only options, "by the law," were death by starvation or murder. Angela wanted to ask her how she felt about the post-humans who would not get a chance to be a part of this new world Kane envisioned, but didn't want to arouse any type of suspicion.

"What's your name?" Angela asked instead.

"Dinah," she said. "What's yours?"

"Angela."

Dinah reached her hand out to shake Angela's, but before she could, her BlackBerry phone made a sound. She looked at a message on her screen and sighed.

"An uncarded person is acting insane. *Shocker.*" Dinah rolled her eyes. "Duty calls," she added before rushing off.

The majority of the people in the room were quiet, all enjoying the melody and the man's smooth vocals. A few visitors lay down on cots, willing to let the music lull them to sleep. Others stayed up late and continued to congregate. While Angela did not understand the majority of topics they discussed, she enjoyed listening to the prayers, thoughts, and conversations. These people were not as preoccupied with saving the world as Jesse and his friends, but the people at the Lighthouse lived a type of quiet resistance. She had the feeling that she could learn just as much here, amongst these thoughtful individuals, than she could inside of the walls of any school. But she didn't have that luxury anymore. She told Violet she appreciated the safe place to stay, but she had to go back to The Resistance tomorrow, no matter the cost. Her father's life was in danger, and Jesse was the only man who could help her find her way back home.

Chapter Sixteen

"Do you want me to come with you?" Violet asked the next morning. Most of the guests were still in the living room, sleeping or chatting. Angela and Violet were sitting at the cocktail table while Winter stood in the nearby kitchen, whipping up breakfast.

Angela was preparing to confront Jesse and Emi to see if either of them would help her find her father, but Winter refused to let anyone leave on an empty stomach. Angela could hear butter sizzling as Winter browned toast over the stove. As Angela watched her cook, she was reminded of her own father cooking dinner back at home. She appreciated the way Winter seemed to enjoy serving others in simple ways, by offering food and shelter to those in need.

"It could be dangerous for you to go alone," Violet said again, drawing Angela's attention back.

"I mean, they did try to lock you away already," Winter agreed from the kitchen.

"I don't really have a choice at this point," Angela said. "The Resistance has cameras everywhere. If I try to bring one of you with me, they will notice, and they have weapons to protect their hideout. I think it's best if I go alone."

"You are forgetting one thing," Violet said. "Jesse and I go way back. And Freedom knows who I am. They won't lay a finger on me. I really want to come with you and make sure you are alright."

"I will be," Angela said. "Once I get back to my father, I can bring him back with me. A place like Lighthouse might do him some good."

Angela tried to picture her father talking about art and philosophy with the members of Lighthouse and chuckled to herself. Maybe he would find a cozy corner and read. Still, at a place like the Lighthouse, Angela got the feeling that that would be okay, too.

"That's a beautiful idea," Violet said. "With your ability to grow food, you could probably start your own Lighthouse."

Angela brushed off Violet's suggestion. "Does Chicago really need more than one? It seems you are already pretty established."

Violet shook her head. "I am talking about starting one *outside* of Chicago. I love your home, Winter, you know I do, but can you imagine a Lighthouse out in the woodlands, away from the Wardens? Angela has the ability to create that."

Winter smiled, "That sounds like a piece of heaven."

"I just want to check on my dad. That's it." Angela said.

Winter offered Angela a plate full of French toast and fruit. It was the best food she had eaten since leaving home. It had been a while since she had felt so full, so loved. But she could not leave her father at home to die. She said goodbye and was on her way.

ANGELA'S HANDS WERE SWEATY AND HER STOMACH was in knots as she approached The Resistance, but she tried not to show her nerves, knowing they were likely already watching her approach. Jesse didn't know she had found her mother's file. Maybe if she acted casual, all would be well.

Angela walked through the broken front door and summoned the loud elevator. When she made it to the basement, Freedom, Rain, Emi and Zinc were already waiting at the elevator door for her.

"Nice of you to join us again, Angela." Freedom's face was hard.

"Sorry, Jesse told me he loved me and it kind of freaked me out," Angela said, careful not to mention her mother's file. "I'm not sure how I feel, and I needed time alone to think."

Freedom stepped closer. She showed no signs of compassion.

"You had a job to do and you failed, Angela," Freedom said. "Only people working for The Resistance can have our CitCard. I'm afraid I'll need that back until you prove yourself."

Angela grimaced, but she handed Freedom the card. Angela knew she would need the card to bring her father back to the settlement. Heck, now even leaving this building could be fatal if a Warden was around. She would need to find a way to get it back before she went to find her father.

"Where is Jesse?" Angela asked.

"He's downstairs, trying to do your job without you," Freedom said. "Come on, follow me."

As Freedom turned away, Angela looked at Emi for help, but she averted her eyes. Angela followed Freedom to the storage room in The City Below. But when Freedom opened the door, Jesse was not inside.

"Where is Jesse?" Angela asked. Freedom ignored

her and grabbed her arm, pulling her inside. Angela let out a high-pitched scream as Freedom's hand roughly clamped over her mouth.

"Quiet," Freedom whispered as she dragged Angela to the dreaded cage reserved for mutants. Reserved for people like her. She was a prisoner, after all, not a guest like she had been led to believe. Freedom had likely ordered Jesse to find her.

As Angela was shoved inside, she cursed herself for being so naive to think she could simply waltz in and convince Jesse to take her back home just because he had said that he "loved" her. Was that all just a trick to get her to come with him? To get her to stay? Freedom locked the cage.

"Let me go!" Angela screamed, her blood boiling with rage.

"I know that you found your mother's file," Freedom said. "And I'm sorry that it has come to this. I know you will not understand this right now, but I am doing this for your own safety. You *cannot* be outside right now."

And with that, Freedom left Angela alone in the room to fiddle with the lock. Tears fell down her face uncontrollably, yet she tried to not make a sound. This was her fault. She had run off, and now her father would die because of her. This was not how any of her fairy tales ever ended. Hours went by and when Angela ran out of tears, she curled into a ball and drifted off to sleep.

THE SOUNDS OF KEYS RATTLING JOLTED ANGELA awake. She sat up in her cage as Emi and Jesse entered the room. Not wanting to get her hopes up, she remained silent.

"Angela!" Jesse raced over to the cage, looking genuinely worried.

"Jesse," Angela walked over to him and smiled, trying to hide her fear and anger. Would he let her out?

"I'm sorry Freedom did this," Jesse said. "We are going to get you out of there."

Angela nodded, hopeful. Emi hung back, letting Jesse do the talking.

"I need to find my father," Angela pleaded. "I think I kept our garden healthy, and without me, I'm sure he will starve. He could already be dead."

"He's not," said Jesse, "but we don't have much time."

"What do you mean?" Angela asked. "Have you seen my father?"

"We just saw him with a group of Wardens. He came to the city looking for you last night and was captured. They are planning another public execution near the market."

Angela felt like the air was being squeezed out of her lungs. She sank to the ground inside of the cage.

"No!" Angela cried out. "Not my father! He didn't do anything wrong."

"But he's not carded," Jesse said. "That's his crime. Don't worry. We are going to get you out of here, and we are going to get your father."

"Freedom took my card," Angela said. Jesse pulled her card out of his pocket and tossed it at her. She caught it as more tears fell. Only this time, they came from a place of joy. There was still time to save her father.

Emi unlocked Angela's cage. Angela took a tentative step out, testing out her newfound freedom. She walked over to the largest gun mounted on the wall and took it down. It felt foreign, cold, and heavy in her hands.

Jesse walked over and took the weapon from her hands. "That's way too much firepower for your first time. Try again."

Angela looked at the many weapons on the wall, trying to find one that would suit her for this rescue mission. Her eyes locked on a long, metal sword that seemed fit for a knight. It reminded her of Excalibur.

Angela walked over to it. She could see her reflection in the blade. As she picked it up, she said, “Let’s bring my father home.”

Chapter Seventeen

The sky was gray and gloomy when Angela, Jesse, and Emi set off towards the market. By the time they approached the old mall in the distance, it was raining hard, and thunder boomed across the skies. Dozens of spectators gathered around the decaying mall, eager to watch the show. In the center of the commotion, three Wardens in their trademark red-, white-, and blue-striped shirts paraded around three prisoners who were shackled together with chains. Even though they were a good distance away, Angela could see that one of the prisoners was her father, but he didn't look how she remembered him. He was thinner and bruised, a hopeless look on his pale, dirty face.

It was all Angela could do not to scream or run to him and say that she was sorry for leaving, that she should have listened and not acted like a child. At the same time, part of her still felt as if he should have known that he couldn't hide her away forever. Why would he stand by while the Watch hunted down her brothers and sisters like dogs? She had come to believe these mutants were her family. Like her, they had been touched by the chaos in the world and still fought to survive.

Angela looked over at Jesse. It didn't matter anymore if he brought her there to use her gift; he was helping her save her father now. She reached out and took his hand.

"I'm sorry, Angela," he said, guilt all over his face. "You were right. Freedom did send me on a mission to find you. She knew about your mother and felt your mutation might be useful. I doubted I would actually find you alive or that you would be so eager to come with me."

"I don't care about any of that right now," Angela said. "How can we save him?"

Jesse looked sternly into Angela's eyes. "We're going to have to kill the Wardens."

"But how?" Angela asked. There was a crowd of thirty people. It would be impossible to kill a Warden in a place like this without being seen.

Angela remembered Jesse promising her that it would not come to this, that she was not here to harm anyone, only to garden. But in this situation, it seemed it was the only way to save her father.

"I don't know, Jesse," Emi said. "We can't do that out in the open like this. Kane will not like the message that it sends. If we do this, every Warden in America will come to Chicago to hunt us down. I do want to help Angela's dad, but maybe this isn't practical."

Angela glared at Emi and Jesse, "So you want to just let my father die?"

Jesse put his hands on Angela's shoulders and looked into her eyes, "It's my fault that either of you are even here. I can't take back the fact that I caused this, but I can keep you safe now. I said I would protect you, and now I am saying that I will protect both you and your father. We are going to save him."

Jesse pulled Emi and Angela behind some debris a safe distance away from the commotion. He waited until both he and Emi had a clear shot.

Angela looked at her sword. "How can I help?"

Jesse chuckled, "Don't bring a knife to a gunfight."

Jesse and Emi fired in unison at the Wardens.

Chapter Eighteen

Emi's bullet flew past the Wardens and crashed into the crumbling walls of the old mall, before ricocheting towards the crowd but hitting no one. However, Jesse was a good shot. His bullet struck the chest of a Warden, causing confusion to flash onto the face of the other two as they looked around to see where the attack came from. One of them looked over at Jesse, Emi, and Angela, and Angela's heart sank as she recognized her familiar face again. The female Warden, Dinah, locked eyes with her. Angela watched her confusion shift to rage.

"Over there!" Dinah called out to her partner. The male Warden turned towards Angela and readied his gun. Angela ducked behind the debris.

Jesse fired again as if their beating hearts were

bull's-eyes. The two Wardens fired as well, and everything was happening so quickly that Angela wasn't sure who had fired first. Bullets struck Dinah and the other Warden. They fell to the ground, victims of Jesse's aim. Before Angela could process that all three wardens were dead, she heard Emi cry out and fall to the ground as well. Angela turned to her friend, seeing blood on the part of Emi's shirt that covered her stomach. At least one of the Wardens had been a good shot, too.

Despite Emi's attempts at providing pressure, the bloodstain grew. Jesse rushed over to Emi, fully embracing her slight frame, forgetting the Watch and the commotion around them, if only for a moment.

Realizing they had a chance to escape death, the prisoners took off running. In their panic and haste to get away, they forgot about the chain that linked them together and fell over each other. Angela ran over to the pile of people on the ground, reaching for her father.

Most of the crowd had run away at the first gunshot, but a few men stood around to yell insults at Jesse and Angela for killing the Wardens. One onlooker lunged at Angela as she tried to help her father to his feet, landing painful blows on Angela's back. Angela pointed the sharp end of her sword at the woman, causing her to back away.

"Back off!" Angela yelled as she led her father and the other two prisoners back to Jesse.

"Murderers!" a man screamed. "Find more Wardens! We need backup!"

It was the first time Angela had considered that the majority of the people in the city didn't hate the Watch. The Watch gave them food and order. To those who were not mutants or un-carded they might seem like saviors, but for the remainder, they were a death sentence.

Jesse pointed his gun towards the man threatening Angela, causing the onlookers to retreat, as well. Angela looked up at her father.

"Daddy!" Angela embraced him. His hair and skin were dirty and he was noticeably skinnier than she remembered. "I'm so glad you are alive!"

"I thought I'd never see you again." Tears fell from her father's eyes. She hugged him, and he did his best to embrace her back, despite the fact that his hands were chained to two other men.

Jesse placed his hand on Angela's shoulder. "We need to get out of here. More Wardens will be here soon."

Jesse's touch pulled Angela's attention away from her father and caused her to look over at Emi. Her body lay motionless, the ground around her covered in blood.

"Emi!" Angela called, rushing over to her friend. She cupped her face, brushing wild blue hair away from her empty eyes. "We need to take her back to Rain. She needs medicine."

"She's gone, Angela," Jesse said. "We need to go. Now."

Jesse pulled Angela up. He looked as if he was holding back tears, but he wouldn't let them fall.

"Now," Jesse repeated.

Before he had a chance to pull her away, Angela picked up Emi's gun.

THEY GUIDED THE PRISONERS BACK TO THE Resistance. It was a slow process that involved taking back roads and trying desperately to avoid the Wardens that were out looking for them.

They took off down an alleyway. Angela lead the way, racing ahead with pistol in hand, while Jesse trailed behind to guard their backs. The three prisoners struggled to coordinate their steps and stumbled over each other. Angela glanced over her shoulder and saw her father cough and wheeze, sweat causing his hair to cling to his skin. Every time she turned to check on him, it looked like he was further behind.

They tried to stay off the beaten path, but people still followed.

"They're over here!" a stranger called out to an unseen Warden.

Jesse pointed his weapon towards the stranger, hoping he would back off, but when that stranger left others came.

The Warden's followed the crowd to discover Angela's location. One emerged ahead of Angela, blocking their path. He pulled out a gun and aimed.

They froze in their tracks. Angela heard Jesse swear under his breath and saw him look back, considering running the other way. But what good is running while a gun is pointed at your back? He dropped his weapon and put his hand up.

The warden sneered at him, approaching quickly, his pistol pointed at Jesse's temple. He picked up Jesse's gun, then turned to Angela.

"Your weapons miss?" there was a condescending tone in his voice. Angela knew the moment they were unarmed they would be killed. Angela slowly lifted her hand to offer him her gun.

While the warden was distracted by the pistol, Angela quickly pulled up her sword and bashed its hilt on the man's head. The man dropped the weapons and fell to the ground. She bashed his head again. As he lay unconscious on the ground, they grabbed all of the weapons and took off running towards the Resistance.

AFTER ANGELA, JESSE, AND THE PRISONERS MADE IT back to headquarters, they took the elevator down into the basement, but no one was there. Angela's heart raced. Had the Wardens gotten there first? How did they even find this place?

"Jesse, is everyone gone?" Angela asked.

"Maybe not," Jesse said, and Angela smiled, realizing that there was one place they still might be.

She took her father and the other two prisoners down into The City Below, cursing herself for willingly venturing back towards the cage.

His instincts proved correct. Freedom, Rain, and Zinc were inside the hidden room. So was Violet, despite Angela's request that she stay behind with Winter. But Violet was the least of Angela's worries now. As soon as Angela walked into the room she lunged at Freedom, shoving her against a wall. Freedom looked stunned that Angela had dared push her.

"How could you lock me up in there?" Angela said. "My father was about to be killed!"

Freedom sighed at Angela. "That's *exactly* why I

locked you away. So you wouldn't run off and get *your-self* killed."

"But it's okay for my father to die, right?" Angela shot back. "I guess his life is worth less because he doesn't have my mutation?"

"I was trying to protect you," Freedom said through gritted teeth.

"We don't have time for this right now," Rain interrupted. "Where's Emi?"

Angela and Jesse said nothing, but the tragedy was written on their faces. Rain was wide-eyed, and Zinc had to take a seat. Even Freedom, usually so stoic, couldn't keep the tears from falling. Angela knew that they understood.

"We did...we did all we could," said Jesse.

"This is why I locked her away," Freedom said.

"Don't blame her. I let her out. And Emi knew the risk when she decided to come."

Freedom nodded, her voice uncharacteristically soft as she replied, "I know."

Freedom worked to get Nathan and the other prisoners out of their chains. The moment her father was free, Angela rushed into his arms sobbing, exhausted. He gave her a full embrace.

"I'm sorry. I'm so sorry," Angela said. "I should have listened to you, I should have never run away."

"I should have never expected to be able to keep

you in one place forever," Nathan said. "I should have told you what you are. This is my fault."

"It doesn't matter who's at fault," Freedom said. "The question is, what do we do next? If you guys did what I heard you did, kill three Wardens in public, they will not relent until they find you."

Jesse used his phone to access the internet. President Kane was live streaming a video across the country, offering rewards for anyone who could find the killers of the Chicago Watch. Everyone watched intently, working themselves into a panic. Eventually, Jesse turned it off.

"They'll raid and raid until they find the ones who did this," Jesse said. "We are not safe in this location, but I have no idea how we could possibly get out of Chicago with the entire settlement, heck the entire country, looking for us. I am the one who killed the Wardens. Maybe if they catch me, they will leave you all alone."

Freedom spoke with force, "The Resistance is a family. While I am furious that you ran off and did this behind my back, you should know that we must stick together. You will not allow yourself to be caught for us."

"If we leave the settlement, who will protect the mutants and the un-carded here?" Rain asked. "We give them food, medicine."

Angela faced Freedom. "They only saw Jesse, Emi, and I. They do not know Zinc, Rain, or you are any part of this. I think you all would still be safe if Jesse and I found a place to hide."

"I'm tired of hiding," Jesse said.

"It's a necessity," Freedom threw back. "Maybe you could go back to Angela's garden? If they were undiscovered there for thirteen years, you should be safe until this dies down."

"No," Angela spoke up. "I have a job here. This is the first place where my gift can be used to help more than just my father and me. My life can't go back to being about just protecting myself."

Freedom rolled her eyes, but Jesse spoke up.

"I agree, Angela," he said. "We are not the first people whose lives have been threatened by the Watch. Maybe at your garden, we can build a new sanctuary."

Violet's eyes grew wide, "A Lighthouse outside of the city? *Now* you're talkin' my language."

"No!" Nathan spoke up. "What will prevent the Watch from coming to my home and killing us all?"

"Look around you, have you seen our armory? We have all we need to keep the place guarded," Jesse promised. "Besides, the Watch only cares about controlling citizens *inside* the settlement. They don't know any habitable land exists outside. When people run out into the forest, they assume we are as good as dead. I doubt they will look for us unless our community gets so big we become a threat. We have some time before we have to worry about that."

"People need more than food and water to live," Angela said. "They need art, beauty, nature, music, hope. If we turn our home into a Lighthouse, we can offer them that."

Nathan nodded slowly, "I guess it would be nice to have a few more people to talk to."

"What about us?" one of the other prisoners, a middle-aged man with bright red hair and a snake tattoo that covered the majority of his face, asked. "Are you just going to send us back out there with the Watch?"

"What's your name," Jesse asked.

"Kevin," he said.

The other prisoner, an athletic-looking, bronze-skinned girl with straight, thick hair, spoke up, "My name is Akeria."

"Our lighthouse already has a few residents," Jesse said. "Come with us."

And with that Jesse walked over to the trap door.

Chapter Nineteen

Jesse pulled the carpet away from the tiny trap door that concealed the entrance to The City Below. He hopped inside, a flashlight in one hand and gun in the other, and smiled up at Violet and the prisoners. Akeria and Kevin looked bewildered. They gawked at him from above.

"The City Below? I thought that was a myth," Kevin said. Akeria nodded in agreement.

"There are no such things as myths," Jesse said, before opening the second door and vanishing into darkness.

Violet's face was visibly pale as she looked into Angela's eyes for assurance. Angela knew how scary it could be to leave home and venture into an unknown world. She reached out and held her friend's hand, hoping to soothe her nerves.

"Lets go," Angela said. "We will build a new Lighthouse there."

Angela and Violet hopped in, followed by Nathan, Kevin, and Akeria. They ventured through the darkness beyond the room that housed the underground garden. Jesse shone his flashlight on a second door that Angela had not noticed before. He pulled the key out of his pocket and opened it. As soon as the door opened, a putrid smell filled the air, causing her to cough and cover her nose.

"My god, that's awful!" Violet exclaimed.

Jesse walked inside, causing the entire party to scramble to keep up with him.

The tunnel beyond this door didn't look much different from the tunnel on the other side. Both were dark, cool, and wet. But this one was much longer, and tiny signs of life reminded Angela that they were not alone. Angela could hear faint sounds echoing from further inside the tunnels — the squeaks of rodents and other unidentifiable forms of life.

"Do you think the Watch could be patrolling down here as well?" Nathan asked. Angela wondered what horrors he had faced in his short time with the Wardens.

"They are the least of your worries down here," Jesse reassured him. "They are concerned with order in the places they rule, once you're outside of their boundaries, they count you as dead. That's why I'm hoping that where you live, we will be left alone."

Angela opened her mouth to respond, but before any words could make it past her lips, a small creature zipped by Angela's feet. It had a rat-like body, but there was something not quite right about its form. Angela squinted at the critter. It was a bit too long to be a rat, with eight tiny legs and two tails moving so effortlessly that its deformities seemed almost correct. Angela screamed in shock.

"Quiet," Jesse said, turning off his flashlight. It was so dark that Angela couldn't see her hands. But it was too late. Angela could hear the distant echo of a much bigger creature approaching. Angela, Jesse, and Violet pressed their backs onto the wall hoping to blend into the darkness. They did their best not to move, or even breathe.

A human-like figure stood in the distance, but due to Jesse's warnings, Angela knew not to assume it was safe. Why would anyone live down here who wasn't forced to? He was tall, and broad across the chest. His breath came heavy and deep as he stood there, watching them.

"Who's there?" he asked. And even though they

could not see him well, they heard the familiar click of a gun preparing to fire. Angela squeezed Jesse's hand, hoping to prevent him from going full cowboy and trying to start a shootout. She had seen enough death for one lifetime.

"I'm warning you!" the man said, and he fired his pistol into the dark. The bullet crashed into the concrete wall.

"Wait!" Angela was the first to speak. "We don't mean any harm. We are trying to get out of here. The Watch is after us."

The man chuckled, "Isn't that why we all end up down here anyway?"

"Can you help us find our way out of the settlement?" Angela asked.

The man grew quiet. Thoughtfully, he spoke, "Leave the settlement? Why, that's a death sentence. You'll die out there in the forest from starvation alone."

"We have plans to make a safe house," Angela spoke up. "We have ways of getting food out there. Medicine, even. Connections with people still living in Chicago. I want to build a community where people like you . . . like us...can live in peace."

The man shone his flashlight to get a good look at Angela and her friends, allowing Angela to do the same to him. He had warm, deep brown skin, close-cropped black, coily hair, and a kind, round face. He looked to be about the same age as Angela's father. His gaze lingered on Angela.

"You sure look familiar," he said.

Jesse stepped between Angela and the man. "She is not from around here. I'm sure you are mistaken."

He sighed at them and put his gun away, but his voice was shaky when he spoke.

"There are some mutants up ahead who don't take kindly to new faces in these parts. We best tread carefully," he said, turning his back on them and taking off. Angela looked over at Jesse, uncertain what to do next.

"Come on!" The man called out. Jesse shrugged at Angela, and they were off with their new guide.

With the man in the lead, they ventured into deeper darkness. They tried to keep their voices to a whisper as they got to know their new friend. His name was Trace, and he had lived in The City Below for fifteen years. Angela felt that was way too long to never see the sunlight. He wasn't a mutant, but his sister was, and the Watch started investigating him for buying medicine that was not prescribed to him. His sister had diabetes, and just because she happened to be a mutant did not mean those issues went away.

"When an adult applies for a CitCard they go

through testing. If it's determined that they have a mutation, they are killed," Trace explained. "Even if she risked applying, during the process they would test her blood for mutations."

Trace broke the law by trying to get insulin for her with his card. A Warden realized what he was doing, but initially let him get away. Later that night, three Wardens raided Trace's home, trying to figure out who the medicine was for. Trace hid his sister in a locked freezer in the basement as the Wardens searched the home. They found nothing, but Trace knew luck had run out for him and his sister. That night, they moved to The City Below.

"Where is your sister now?" Angela asked.

"She died, thirteen years ago," he said. "From her illness, not from any mutation. It was hard getting the meds she needed down here. Some carded people from above ground tried to help us as much as they could, but you know how it is. I think most of them ended up getting mutations themselves. You can't buy meds without citizenship cards. Up there, they would have killed her even sooner. It's always been a situation where you can't win, but I'm glad she got a couple extra years of life down here."

"I'm sorry, that's awful," Angela said. Everyone she knew had faced so much loss. Even though

Angela grew up without her mom, she felt guilty for being shielded from so much pain.

"You know, you look kind of like her," Trace said.

"Like your sister?" Angela asked.

"No, like one of the women who helped us get meds when we first moved underground. Good friend of mine. Her name was Aliyah"

Angela's heart pounded. She looked over at her father, trying to read his expression in the dark.

"Aliyah," her father said to Trace, too stunned to say anything else.

Angela pulled her mother's photograph out of her pocket, asking, "Was this the woman you knew?"

Trace took the photo and gave it a quick look. "Yes, that's her. We grew up going to the same school our whole life. When my sister mutated, a lot of our friends left us, but not her. One of the kindest women I knew. You know, she had a mutation as well, but not as noticeable as some. Last time I saw her, she said she was going someplace secret to be cured."

"We tried so many cures," Nathan said, a tear slipping down his face.

Trace looked at Angela with warmth in his eyes. He walked over to her and put his arm on her shoulder. "I don't even have to ask, you are the spitting image of her. Know that your mother was a good woman, brave and resilient. She cared about the people the world overlooked. I can see that her spirit lives on through you," Trace said.

Angela couldn't help herself. She wrapped her arms around the man and concentrated on not sobbing into this stranger's shirt.

"If I'm going to help you all, I will need to arm myself with more than just this pistol," Trace said, hugging her back. "I know a place where we can get some supplies. Come on."

Trace shone his flashlight down the dark hallway and started to lead the group through the tunnels. Eventually, they could hear the chatter and laughter of various voices in the distance. The voices sounded free and open, but Trace warned his new friends to be cautious.

"Hello!" he called out ahead. "Customers approaching. Some new faces here."

They turned the corner to find a room illuminated in dim yellow lights, the low hum of a power generator was the only sound as twelve silent faces looked Trace's guests over with curiosity. About half of them had visible mutations. Most were a little too hairy or unusual to pass as normal. Beyond the physical differences in clientele, this shop was similar to the market inside the old mall — a place for people to gather and barter.

Two figures stood tall over all others. They looked

like men, but their pale skin had a greenish tint, and they had such extreme height and muscle mass that Angela was sure they must have some type of mutation. These imposing men did not speak.

"I ain't seen you in these parts," said a bald, pale man that Angela had not noticed before. At his feet, a large alligator rested. Its yellow eyes blinked at Angela.

"Their goods work just as well as the people you see all the time," Trace responded.

The man looked them over once more before speaking.

"Name's Al. Mess with me, you mess with my best friend, Allie, right here," he said, pointing at the creature at his feet.

"Not a problem," Trace said, stocking up on weapons and ammo. Al did not charge any money, but Trace traded a few items to get what he needed. Jesse traded some extra ammo to buy additional food and water for the group. He figured they would need it once they made it above ground.

When Trace decided they had enough supplies to get out in one piece, they were on their way again.

Most of the journey was uneventful. They ran into mutants, but the majority were nonviolent. Trace told stories about his sister and cool secrets about The City Below. He also shared memories of Angela's mother from his childhood growing up with her in the same south Chicago high school. Trace's stories about her mother were the first stories that Angela loved even more than fairy tales. Angela got the feeling that he had been alone for a while and he enjoyed having people to talk to. So much so, that he was willing to risk his life for the company.

"Wait," Trace whispered, pausing in his tracks as they walked through the tunnels. "I hear something up ahead."

Angela could hear it too, the faintest laugh echoing in the distance. Trace pointed his flashlight forward.

There were five of them ahead, standing perfectly still like tall, thin statues. Their skin was the palest white, almost translucent, and their eyes were an icy blue. Their hair, long and gray, clung to the sweat on their necks. Their clothes were both wet and dirty, and their feet were bare. One of them, the smallest of the bunch and the only female, smiled a wide, toothless grin and moved towards the group; a quick, swift movement that reminded Angela of a cat leaping towards its prey. They held no weapons, and as Jesse pointed his gun towards them, they were not fazed. Angela wondered why these mutants were so fearless.

"Don't come any closer," Jesse called out. Their only response was to laugh. The shrill sound echoed through the tunnel and caused Angela to shiver. In the blink of an eye, the pale girl's face was inches away from Angela's, her eyes wide and her grin menacing. Angela shrieked and stepped back, but not quickly enough to prevent the girl from reaching out and grabbing Angela's arm, causing her to cry out in pain.

The pale girl's skin was colder than ice, so cold that Angela felt as if her arm was starting to freeze over. In the light of Trace's flashlights, Jesse could visibly see the blue veins under Angela's brown skin rise, pronounced and frozen like icicles. Jesse fired a round at the mutant girl's pale arm, causing her to giggle rather than retreat. She lifted her other hand to Angela's neck, and the chill from the slightest touch made it difficult for Angela to breathe. This caused Jesse to fire straight through the pale girl's heart. She fell to the ground as Angela gasped for air, and Jesse noticed that the pale girl, though dead, did not bleed. He had never encountered this type of mutation before.

In the blink of an eye, all of the pale girl's friends were inches away, ready to attack. Trace and Jesse fired as many rounds as they could at the creatures, but it was Angela's sword that stopped a creature in its tracks as it tried to reach for Jesse's neck. Angela stabbed the sword into the creature's belly and watched as it fell to the ground.

"Thank me later," Angela said to Jesse. He couldn't help but smile at her as he fired a round into another mutant that was reaching for Angela's father. Angela glanced over at Violet, who seemed to be enjoying herself as she zapped every mutant that got close to her.

Once the creatures were all dealt with, the remainder of the trek to the exit was quick. Jesse pointed out a rusted metal ladder leading out of the tunnels.

"I hope you guys make it out of the settlement safely," Trace said, a sad smile on his face. "You are some brave ones, as far as land-dwellers come."

"Would you like to come with us?" Angela asked. "We have room for one more friend where we're going."

Angela looked over at her father, expecting him to protest, but instead her father smiled.

"Really?" Trace asked. "Are you sure it won't be a problem?"

"Not at all," Angela said. "It would be nice to have someone of your skills helping us out for the rest of our journey. And I would love to learn more about your childhood with my mother on the way there. We still have a long way to go."

Trace beamed at them. "I guess that will be alright. Don't get me wrong, I love moldy, wet, smelly underground tunnels, but I'm due for a change of scenery," he said, shining his light on the ladder that headed to the exit hatch.

Angela grabbed the cool metal bar on the ladder and climbed up and out.

Chapter Twenty

When Angela and her friends emerged from the tunnels, they found themselves at an abandoned L train stop on the outskirts of Chicago. Angela traced her fingers over letters on a nearby sign.

"Lake," Angela said, remembering the word from her sight word lessons with Miss Kaper. Nathan looked over at Angela, surprise in his eyes.

"Did you just read?" he asked.

"Of course," Angela said with a shrug. "If you thought sword fighting and gun slinging were the only things I've been up to, then you don't know your daughter. I have your entire bookshelf to devour once I get back home."

"Harlem/Lake," Jesse said, looking around in amazement. "This is near my old stomping grounds.

My family lived in Oak Park back in the day, and my grandparents lived up here. My God, so much has changed. It's a ghost town now."

Trace looked towards the bright yellow moon and stars and took a deep breath.

"I thought I'd never see the stars again," he said.

While they were technically still within the boundaries of the settlement, it was clear no one had lived this close to the edge for some time. The homes and businesses had all been reduced to rubble, and no people hung out so far from the settlement center. There were no Wardens patrolling this area, but the forest was still a distant walk. Covered by the dark night sky, they set off towards home.

Despite Nathan's constant worries about mutants, the only problem they ran into was tired feet. In all honesty, Angela was starting to doubt very many human mutants truly lived in the wild. It was much easier to get food in The City Below. Then again, maybe they were just good at hiding.

The journey back home felt even longer to Angela than her journey to the settlement. It took Angela a full seven days to ask her father the question that had been in the back of her mind.

"Daddy, you are my biological father, right?" Angela asked.

"Of course," he said, concerned. "Why on earth would you ask me that?"

"I don't look like you," Angela said.

"You are the spitting image of your mother," he said, dipping his hand into his pocket and pulling out a small locket. He opened it, revealing a photo of Angela as a baby, being held by Aliyah, with Nathan smiling on as he wrapped his arms around his wife.

"I'm glad you are," Angela said. "But even if you weren't, it wouldn't change anything. I love you. Thank you for coming after me to bring me home."

When Angela finally saw her home in the distance, she didn't immediately recognize it. The garden looked just as dry and barren as the rest of the forest. There were no plants or food, and the stream was murky, low and still. However, Angela's heart skipped a beat when she saw her piano sitting outside of the cottage. Angela hadn't realized how much she missed her music until now.

Despite the barren land, this was home. Only now, Angela and her father had others to share it with and a mission to help create a place of healing within the struggling world. Angela's father walked up behind her and put his hands upon her shoulders. She looked up at him and smiled, squeezing his hand tight.

Violet stepped into the garden gate and started exploring.

"So this is paradise, huh?" she asked.

"It looked much different last time I saw it," Angela said. "We are going to have to work to get it back to the way that it was. Even with my gift, it will take time."

Nathan sighed, "It's definitely going to take some time to get this place back to how it was."

"It needs to be better than it was before if we are bringing more people here," Jesse said. "Safer, more secure. The Watch will not care if a few rogue people are living in the wild, but as a community, they might see us as a threat."

Jesse started to brainstorm possible security strategies. He talked about building a basement under Angela's home to hide if the Watch ever showed up and building a couple of additional cabins to house people. He suggested he might be able to travel back to the settlement occasionally to keep communications open with Winter and Freedom.

"Let's give this place a name," Violet said. "I think Lighthouse is a little too bland for a place like this."

"How about Eden?" Nathan spoke up.

"I like it," Violet exclaimed.

"Well, I'm ready to turn this place into a home," Trace said. "What should we do first?"

Both Jesse and Nathan opened their mouths to answer, but Angela interrupted them by taking off towards her piano.

"This," she answered Trace's question by brushing off the dirt and grime collected on its bench. She plopped down, letting her fingers find their familiar resting places on the keys. She looked towards her father, "I learned a new song."

Angela played the tune she had heard at Lighthouse by ear, singing the lyrics as best as she could remember.

"I'M JUST A POOR WAYFARING STRANGER
Traveling through this world below
There is no sickness, no toil, nor danger
In that bright land to which I go"

TO ANGELA'S SURPRISE, NATHAN STARTED TO SING along. Violet, who knew all the words, belted out the song while Jesse, Trace, Kevin, and Akeria started to hum the melody. While music had always given her peace, the feeling was compounded as she listened to their voices blending together. Angela smiled, realizing that even though she wasn't living in the settlement, she had finally found a community. Jesse sat beside her on the bench, putting his arm around her waist as she played. She lay her head on his shoulder, realizing that she made more than simply a new friend in Jesse.

Angela looked around the garden as her fingers hit the keys, taking in the familiar sights. She knew restoring a thirty-acre garden would take time. However, she couldn't shake the feeling that the garden was already changing, as she stood with her friends and sang, into more of a home than it had ever been. Maybe it was all in Angela's mind, but when she looked around the garden, the grass already seemed a little greener.

Acknowledgments

This book would not be possible without the support of others. I received helpful feedback from people in online writing communities such as Black Girls Belong in Fantasy and Sci-Fi Writers Society and Writers Helping Writers. I would like to thank my husband, Justin McEntire, for making sure I was fed and hydrated while binge typing, and my parents, Keith and Janet Smith, because they read my books when they were written in crayon and held together by staples and they always believed in my story.

Credits

Cover Design: MoorBooks Design
Editor: Ibis Literary
Layout: Pixie Covers

K. R. S. McEntire (Keshia McEntire) shares all of her bookish finds on her Facebook page "Diverse Fantasy and Sci-Finds." Connect with her by searching @DiverseFSF.

Made in the USA
San Bernardino, CA
21 January 2020